MOUSE INVADERS
THE EXCITING ESCAPADES OF ARVEE THE MOUSE

'Magnolia' is the pen-name of writer and artist Manjula Padmanabhan. She grew up in Europe and South East Asia. Her comic strip, 'Sukiyaki', appears weekly in *Business Line*, Chennai. Aside from books for grown-ups, she has published a number of books for children as author–illustrator. She lives in the US with no cats, plants or children.

Other books by Magnolia

MOUSE ATTACK
The Amazing Adventures of Arvee the Mouse

MOUSE INVADERS

THE EXCITING ESCAPADES
OF ARVEE THE MOUSE

written and illustrated by

MAGNOLIA

hachette
INDIA

First published in 2004 in hardback by Macmillan Children's Books
First published in paperback in 2005 by Macmillan Children's Books
A division of Macmillan Publishers Ltd
20 New Wharf Road
London N1 9RR Basingstoke and Oxford
Associated companies throughout the world
www.panmacmillan.com

First published in India in 2019 by Hachette India
(Registered name: Hachette Book Publishing India Pvt. Ltd)
An Hachette UK company
www.hachetteindia.com

1

This is a work of fiction.
Any resemblance to real persons or animals, living or dead, or actual events or locales
is purely coincidental.

ISBN 978-93-88322-33-1

Hachette Book Publishing India Pvt. Ltd
4th & 5th Floors, Corporate Centre
Plot No. 94, Sector 44, Gurugram - 122003, India

Typeset in Georgia 11/15.8 by
by Manmohan Kumar, Delhi

Printed and bound in India
by Manipal Technologies Limited, Manipal

CONTENTS

PROLOGUE:
A FORMIDABLE ENEMY

On a fine February morning, Ellie Stringer sat in the flowering bush that grew above her home in the Lantana Mouse Enclave. Sunlight filtering down through the leaves sparkled in her whiskers. She twiddled her sensitive nose this way and that, enjoying the rich bouquet of scents brought to her by the fresh breeze. *Mmm!* she thought to herself. *That's the yellow roses . . . the dandelions . . . the nasturtiums . . . and a very young butterfly drying its wings in the sun and. . . oooh! Yuck!*

She stopped suddenly. Among all the colourful and friendly fragrances, there was one rather horrid one. Ellie frowned. It seemed very far away. She breathed in and out sharply a few times to clear the memory of the stink, then leaned back against the lantana's flower stem with its bunches of little florets, pink and white. On her lap was a blank Scrabble tile, which she was using as a writing tablet. On the tablet was a pale yellow Post-it note, folded over to make a mouse-sized notebook. Using a bit of pencil lead, Ellie began a note to her best friend, Arvee.

'HELO RV', she wrote. 'PLIZ FORGIV MY SPELING. THIS IZ MY FURST TRY AT RITING TO U. OR TO ENNY ONE. WAIR R U I WUNDER.' There was so much she wanted to tell him! But, 'IT IZ VERI HARD TO RITE,' she said, 'SO I MUST STOP.'

She pencilled in the final 'P' and leaned back once more. Arvee was away on a world tour with his human family. He'd already been gone for three months. At least another three remained before his return. Since there was no way for them to communicate, her note would only reach him when he got back. Writing to him was the closest she could get to talking to him! She was just about to attempt expressing that thought in written words when she heard, in the distance, a thin shriek.

She sat up, all her senses alert. It had sounded like a young mouse's cry for help. Even as she scrambled to get to her paws, hastily tucking the Scrabble tile and Post-it note into her cloth shoulder bag, she heard mouse voices raised in alarm. The unpleasant smell came again. Stronger this time. It was still far away, but it smelt of something rotten, ugly and . . . mean.

Ellie's heart began to hammer in her small chest, causing the delicate outspread membranes of her ears to tremble. The frightened cries had risen in volume and number. And now there was another sound. A dry, slithering rustle. Something big was moving beneath the lantana bushes. Something low on the ground. Something moving fast. Ellie was breathing in short gasps, frozen where she stood. She hardly knew why she was so afraid, yet her body was reacting from an instinctive knowledge of the enemy heading straight towards her.

The Lantana Mouse Enclave had been formed under an orderly row of lantana bushes, some fifteen of them, at the front end of Paradise Villa's luxurious garden. The bushes were sandwiched between the emerald-green expanse of the lawn and the red-brick boundary wall of the property. A vast bougainvillea creeper frothed down over the wall, while a barricade of thorny euphorbias in big square pots stood between the lawn and the pretty flowering lantanas.

The cry for help had come from the bush furthest from where Ellie sat. That's where the stench had come from too. Now the rustling sound was approaching from that same direction. Ellie wanted desperately to jump up and run. But from the tip of her nose to the end of her tail, she was paralysed with terror. Closer and closer came the rustling until, abruptly, it stopped. There was a silence. Then the rustling began again, but moving upwards. Two bushes away, the leaves began to quiver. Ellie stared, her eyes wide with terror, as her worst nightmare rose slowly into view.

It was a young cobra, handsome and deadly. Dapples of sunlight glittered upon the shiny black scales of its head and down the creamy-white length of its throat. Its wicked jaws were half-open. Between them lay the tiny, motionless body of a baby mouse.

1

TOP SECRET

Three Months Later – Thursday Morning

The sun was just beginning to peep over the horizon. Ten-year-old Mo flopped gratefully on to her bed, tired out from her long journey. 'Good morning, Arvee,' she called out to him sleepily. 'Or do I mean goodnight?'

'Goodnight, Mo,' Arvee replied, even though he knew she didn't understand his speech. He was a white mouse after all, and very few human children knew his language. Not many adults did either, for that matter.

He, Mo and her parents had just returned to their home in New Delhi. They lived in a house called Paradise Villa. Arvee had a mouse-sized mansion called *Mercara* all to himself. It stood on top of a round table in a small chamber just next to Mo's bedroom.

Arvee listened till he was sure that his young human friend was sound asleep, then, using the escape hatch he'd cut through the floor of his living room and the table-top, he scrambled down to the floor. Tiptoeing across Mo's room, he reached the door that led to the veranda. It was normally shut tight, but this morning, in order to air the house, the maid had propped the door open and gone away.

Just inside the door to the room was Arvee's brand-new, all-terrain Mouse-Deluxe bike. Leaping on to it, he kicked it off its stand and launched himself across the veranda. In a twinkling, he had reached the three steps that led towards the garden. He bumped down on to the steps. Thank goodness they were shallow! *Bump-ta . . . bump-ta . . .* and then a final bump. Moments later, he was pedalling furiously along the red sandstone path leading from Paradise Villa towards the boundary wall along which the lantana bushes grew.

He was, of course, forbidden to leave the house at any time. He knew perfectly well that it wasn't safe for a mouse to be out in the garden. Not even a scholarly pet mouse like himself, a scientist with a pedigree as long as his tail and a houseful of human friends. There were crows, for instance, who wouldn't mind taking a swipe at him. There were rough-mannered stray cats who sometimes wandered in. Occasionally there was even a dog or two, venturing in from other bungalows in the neighbourhood.

All the same, Arvee knew, as he raced towards the front end of the garden, he just *had* to take the risk. He might never get another such chance again. During all that time he'd been away, he'd had no news of his friends Ellie, Toon and the rest of the house mice he'd grown so close to the previous year. Following the disastrous flood that had ruined Paradise Villa's foundations, all the creatures living in the house had been forced to move into the garden. Before his departure Arvee had spent all his spare time helping his friends adjust to life out of doors.

Once he'd left, however, there was no way of remaining in touch with them. They had no electricity and their radio sets had been ruined by the flood. Postcards would have been an option if his friends had known how to read and write. But they didn't. So for six months he and they had had to endure a long unbroken silence.

Arvee braked hard as he reached the end of the red flagstones. The first of the euphorbia pots was right next to the path. Beyond it lay the lantana bushes. Lifting his bike down on to the bare earth near the pots, he was about to jump back on and pedal towards Ellie's house at the other end of the Enclave when, 'Ahem!' said someone very loudly.

Arvee looked up.

Standing under the shade of the closest euphorbia pot was a stranger. He was a garden shrew, an altogether shorter and more streamlined animal than a mouse. He had, like others of his kind, a blunt tail, a pointed, twitchy nose, small black eyes and almost invisible ears. His fur was grey and shiny, lying flat against his skin, as if oiled down. In addition, this particular shrew was dressed in something like a military uniform. He wore a half-sleeved shirt and shorts in dark brown cloth with patches of green and black. There was a whistle on a string dangling from his neck. From his belt hung a baton. On his head, attached by a length of twine, he wore a cap fashioned out of an almond shell. On his feet were sturdy boots, beetle-wing black and well polished.

'Heh-heh – oh, my!' said the stranger, snickering in the way of someone who is uncomfortable but wants to conceal it. 'There's only one animal you can be . . . the famous Professor Arvee. That's who you are, yes?' He didn't offer Arvee a paw to shake. 'Heh-heh – pleased to meet you I'm sure! The name's Diss. Neighbourhood Security Officer Diss. Now then. Want to see your – heh-heh – friends, do you?'

'Well, uh – yes,' stammered Arvee. He was so taken aback that he couldn't focus on what Officer Diss was saying to him. 'I've been away, you see, and I really want to meet them – '

'Heh-heh, of course you do,' said the garden shrew. 'Sad to say, however, NOT POSSIBLE!' He did not seem the least bit sad, though.

'What!' said Arvee, forgetting his manners. 'That is, uh, do you mean they're . . . Uh, are they all right? Or have they moved?'

'Heh-heh – can't tell you!' said Diss. 'Top secret, that. Whereabouts of residents of Lantana Mouse Enclave. Meanwhile, you're the one who's not officially present, see? Got to be registered. Can't move around the Lantana Mouse Enclave without the proper papers. And you don't have 'em. Do you?' He crinkled his little eyes in a falsely jovial way. 'Thought not. Heh-heh. Takes a week to get all the permissions in order. Goodbye!' With that he prepared to turn on his heel and go away.

'Wait!' spluttered Arvee. 'You can't – I mean – you've not explained anything!' Nothing like this had ever happened before. 'I just need to see Ellie right away, you know, and then I can – '

'Sorry!' called Diss over his shoulder, as he sauntered away into the shade under the euphorbia pot. 'Can't break the rules! Even for a Very Important Mouse like you. Make a proper application. Then we'll see.' And he was gone.

Arvee was stunned. He smoothed back his whiskers. The sun was hot on his sparkling white fur and dazzling to his ruby-pink eyes, despite the protective goggles he wore against the glare. His heart had been so set on seeing Ellie right away! The idea of waiting a week was . . . unthinkable. Not only that, but the shrew had given no indication of how to make an application.

Arvee had grown up in a laboratory. He knew about Due Procedure and Filling in Forms and Following Rules. He also knew that forms, procedures and rules were sometimes ways of saying 'no', without having to offer explanations.

This seemed to be one of those times.

He took a deep breath.

Leaping on to the saddle of his bike, he pumped his paws, not looking left or right, making for the lantana bushes. Almost instantly, he heard a startled squawk from Diss, then the sound of a whistle being blown furiously and small booted feet attempting to give chase. But the mouse was going much too fast for the shrew to catch up. Within seconds, the Neighbourhood Security Officer was left far behind as Arvee raced towards Ellie's house.

2

JUST LIKE OLD TIMES

Thursday Morning

Arvee streaked through the colony at a blistering pace. He splashed through a small puddle of water, disturbing a squadron of gnats settled upon its surface. He almost ran over the tail of a sleepy earthworm. He tinkled his bell furiously at two elegant snails blocking his path – they paid no attention to him, of course, as they had no ears, so he had to slalom round them carefully before setting off again.

Finally he was at the Stringer family's door. Like the rest of the mice in the Enclave, Ellie's family lived in an underground cabin. All that showed above ground was a modest mound of earth with a carefully concealed door set into it. Arvee's ears were bright pink with the exertion of his ride. He leapt down from his bike, put it on its stand, smoothed back his whiskers and reached for the bell-pull. This was a shiny knob, made from the tip of a staghorn beetle's antler, hanging at the end of a length of embroidery thread from a low branch. One-two-three, he pulled, one-two-three. Ellie would know it was him!

His whiskers quivering with impatience, he waited a couple of seconds . . . then five, then ten. Was it possible the bell wasn't working? He tried the bell again. No response.

He looked behind himself nervously. He knew that Officer Diss would eventually catch up with him and, when he did, would undoubtedly make an awful nuisance of himself. Ten more seconds crawled by and still there was no sign of movement from behind the silent little door of Ellie's house. Arvee wondered if he should risk ringing the bell a third time.

He had just about made up his mind to try again when, to his great relief, the door opened. 'Ellie!' he cried. 'Oh, I'm so gl – '

But he couldn't continue. His friend was looking too worried to greet him properly.

'Quick!' she said. 'Get inside! Or you'll be seen.'

'By that officious little shrew I met at the boundary of Lantana Enclave, you mean?' asked Arvee, as he stepped inside the door. 'Nibberty Sickerty Diss?'

Ellie smiled at that. Then she locked the door securely behind Arvee. For a moment, the worried expression was wiped clear from her pretty and cheerful face. 'Oh dear,' she said, 'if he's met you, that means he'll be here any minute, wanting all kinds of. . .' But, glancing up, she gave a sudden grin. 'Ohh, *Ar*-vee! It's *so* nice to have you back! It almost gives me hope that everything will be all right again!' she said.

They exchanged big hugs, then made their way down the stairs.

'What do you mean?' Arvee wanted to know.

But Ellie held a finger to her mouth. 'Please. I'll tell you about it later,' she whispered. 'My parents don't like to hear any of it.'

Ellie's parents, Stringer and Ding, were standing at the foot of the stairs, their faces beaming with pleasure at the sight of Arvee. After a volley of hugs and counter-hugs he was shown into the drawing room, where the baby of the family, Moon Bum or Moonie, as he was known, was toddling about unsteadily on plump baby paws. Even Stringer's father, Oldmouse Stringer, looked up dreamily from where he sat in a rocking chair. He was very frail, and it was never clear how much he understood of what was happening around him. Nevertheless, he did look in Arvee's direction with what seemed like a smile twinkling in the depths of his white whiskers.

The four mice settled down to drink mugs of steaming herb tea in the cheery drawing room. With so much news to share, for the first half an hour the air was filled with 'Oh, and you should have seen – ' and 'I thought of you when – '

Stringer was starting to make a name for himself as an avant-garde furniture designer and clearly enjoyed his work. All around the room were samples of his craft: a coffee table made from the lens of a magnifying glass, with clusters of straight pins as legs; and a room divider made from ballpoint-pen refills, woven together with multicoloured embroidery threads; a handsome chest of drawers created from a discarded printer cartridge.

'Remember how we used to make shelves out of matchboxes in the old drainpipe house?' he said to Arvee. 'Well, when we came here, I needed a material that wouldn't succumb to damp and rot. That's when I had the idea of carving plastic items, using one of those marvellous blades you found for me, Arvee.' He had fashioned excellent chisels and knives out of discarded segments of box-cutter blades.

Ding, meanwhile, had become an avid farmer. She grew mushrooms in the cellar of the house and cultivated many varieties of grasses for their seeds. These she ground up as baking flour. She reared aphids for the sweetish milk-like secretions they produced at certain phases in their life cycle, using it for making custards and toffees. 'You must have a meal with us soon,' she said to Arvee. 'I can't wait to try out my latest creations on you!' In addition, there was always a fresh supply of succulent caterpillars and grubs for the table, based on Ding's precise knowledge of where to find the eggs left by butterflies and moths, which ones would develop into what kinds of caterpillars, and how many she could safely remove without harming the creatures' long-term survival prospects.

'I've become a general-purpose teacher and crèche-manager!' said Ellie, laughing. 'I gather up all the children in the neighbourhood and take them out on nature walks. We learn what we can about the plants around us, and the beetles, the midges, the worms and the grubs . . .' She shook her head ruefully. 'Of course, I'm always aware of how little I know, compared to how much there is to learn.'

'The very best of teachers,' said Arvee, 'are those who realize they can never learn enough. I'm sure you're wonderful!' He beamed at her, then turned around to include her parents as he said, 'You can't imagine how happy I am to be back! All the amazing and exciting things I saw and did on my journey were only amazing or exciting because I knew I could come back to tell all of you about them!'

He had been to Japan, he said, where he learned to fly moth-wing kites and to eat his food with chopsticks made from hedgehog bristles. He had been to China and learned how to make his own noodles from rice flour.

'It's all in the twist of the wrist,' he said, demonstrating the technique. 'I'm sure Ding could pick it up in two shakes of a cricket's wing – oh, and speaking of crickets, did you know that in China the humans use them for telling the future? Isn't that the funniest thing?'

All the mice laughed, because they knew exactly how giddy and unreliable crickets were.

The stories went on and on. At last Arvee said, 'I brought lots of presents back with me, but they're still packed away in my luggage. I had to grab my chance to leave the room while the outer door was open.' Saying this reminded him that he should be getting back to Mo and to *Mercara*.

A pall fell over the room, as if a curtain had been drawn across the pleasant, friendly atmosphere that had filled it till then. 'It's not easy any more, getting in and out of Paradise Villa,' said Stringer, 'I've been there with Toon and the others to check out the renovation work. All our old passageways and escape routes have been plugged!'

Toon was his nephew. Along with his group of young rebels, he had been at the forefront of the struggle the previous year to win freedom from the criminal rat gang that had taken over the human house.

'Toon!' exclaimed Arvee. 'My goodness, where is he? And how are all the rest of the gang – Horse, Lucky, Heavy, Happy, Feather, Willing, Zero?'

Stringer scratched the fur between his ears before answering. Both Ellie and Ding were looking away. 'Ah –

you know what the boy's like! And the rest of the gang with him. Incurably restless. All that team from the old Ratland days, they don't live in Lantana Enclave any more. They've taken over an abandoned squirrel's nest in the big neem tree. You know, the one that dominates the lower half of the garden? They're up to all sorts of experiments and escapades out there.'

Ding said, 'We don't see them as much as we'd like to. They seem well enough.'

Arvee glanced across at Ellie and saw that she was looking down at her paws. The set of her ears told him that there was something she'd like to add but was holding back for the time being. It was only now, at least one hour since he'd set eyes on her, that he noticed she wasn't wearing her customary pink scarf round her shoulders any more. Instead, she had on a dark brown blouse over a military grey skirt, long and full. All the mice, he realized suddenly, were wearing sober colours. It wasn't at all like them. Especially not Ellie, who loved sunny yellows and happy reds. Arvee was the most gaily dressed among them, with his electric-blue T-shirt, his white jeans and a snazzy new pair of trainers, made of a transparent material that glowed in the dark.

That's when he remembered his bike.

'Oh!' he cried, giving the other mice a start, 'I've been so thrilled to be back with you that I clean forgot to mention my most recent obsession!' He jumped to his feet, laughing at himself. 'You'd never imagine, considering that I've not mentioned it even once in the past hour, the extent to which this thing has completely taken over my life. You've just got to come up and look – I left it by the door – and no, I'm not going to tell you what it is until you've seen it.'

His enthusiasm was infectious, even though an uneasy glance passed between Ellie and her mother. The other mice got to their paws.

Ellie said, 'I didn't realize you'd left something outside.'

Arvee grinned. 'Just you wait till you see it!' He raced up the stairs.

But Ellie was close behind him. When they got to the top, she darted forward, saying, 'Er – Arvee, please, I think it'll be best if I go out ahead of you, just in case.'

He shrugged and smiled as he held the door open for her.

She stepped out in front of him, automatically turning her head this way and that, looking for something that might startle and delight her. In the split second before Arvee followed her out, a dreadful premonition came to him. It was like a white-hot skewer puncturing the innermost membrane of his being, leaving him exposed, like a beetle on a dissection table: the fear that his precious, gleaming, swift-as-the-wind, six-gear, all-terrain bike would not be there.

An instant later, standing outside the entrance to the Stringer family home, looking at the place where he so clearly remembered setting his beloved machine on its stand, the screaming sensation in the pit of his stomach solidified into a hard, black ball.

The bike, indeed, was gone.

Meanwhile, strolling leisurely up towards them, was Neighbourhood Security Officer Diss. On his face was a satisfied smirk.

3

RULES AND REGULATIONS

Thursday Mid-morning

'Keep him busy for a moment,' hissed Ellie to Arvee. She whipped around and went back through the door. 'There's something I've got to fetch.'

The shrew drew level with Arvee. 'So!' he said, his moist pointy nose wobbling like a blob of pinkish-grey jelly. 'Heh-heh-heh. Not so fast after all, eh? Not even the great Professor Arvee can escape the law. Oh, no.'

Arvee wished he knew what to say that would wipe the nasty smile off the other animal's snout, but he realized it was best to remain neutral for the time being. 'Can't imagine what you mean,' he muttered.

'I'll show you soon enough,' said Diss, oily with exaggerated politeness, 'if you'll be kind enough to follow me.'

'Where to?'

'Why,' said the shrew, 'to the same place all common criminals go – the lock-up!'

At that moment, Ellie reappeared. She was panting slightly from running up the stairs two at a time. Stepping quickly between Arvee and Diss, she said, 'Ah – no, that won't be necessary, sir. I'll vouch for this mouse. He's known to me.'

The shrew's face soured immediately and his beady eyes drew close together as he frowned. 'Nonsense! You know the rules, Miss – '

'Yes, I do – I've learned them by heart, just like you have, I'm sure. *Every animal must either be registered or else always be personally vouched for by another animal*,' said Ellie. 'That's what I'm doing.'

'Personal vouching is invalid unless – '

'. . . *there's an ant for your records*,' said Ellie patiently. 'Yes, I know. Here it is.' Holding up her paw, she showed the shrew a small wire cage. Inside it, Arvee saw, was an ant. 'I've personally coached the ant. I've had it ready for some time, in preparation for whenever Arvee returned. Plus the registration fee: one flat, white, pearly, four-hole button. Attached to the base of the cage.' She looked Officer Diss calmly in the eye. 'I believe you'll find everything's in order, Officer.'

The shrew's long thin nose trembled with frustration. He couldn't think up any reason on the spur of the moment to deny that she was right. 'Huh! Irregular, that's what I call it. Irregular and secretive. You've not explained how you knew he was due to visit, have you? Oh, yes. Irregular and secretive. Two things we disapprove of here in the Lantana Mouse Enclave. Oh, and wait!' A thought occurred to him. 'What about the speeding? Driving in a Wild and Reckless Manner, ho yes, upon an un'hauthorized bi-cyclator – '

'Bi-cyclator?' asked Ellie, with her eyebrows raised. 'What's that, Officer?'

Diss stopped short and gulped a few times. 'Errgle . . . errgle . . . hrrumph,' he said.

The offending machine was nowhere in sight. Of course it wasn't. He had confiscated it himself, having followed Arvee to the Stringer family's doorstep a short while ago. The bicycle had been parked invitingly out in the open. Right then and there, he'd had the idea of wheeling it quietly away, before pretending it had been his all along. Such a gadget could be supremely useful to a law enforcer such as himself. Once he'd taught himself to ride it, that is.

'He means my bicycle,' explained Arvee to Ellie. 'It's the thing I wanted to show you.' The shock of losing it was starting to fade. 'It was parked right here. It's been impounded, I suppose?'

'Err . . . yes,' said Diss, gnashing his teeth. He could hardly claim that the machine belonged to him while charging the wretched albino mouse for driving it recklessly! 'Impounded until further notice – '

'Unless we collect it before sunset on the day of its confiscation,' countered Ellie. 'Section Four of the Snatched Goods Law. Come on, Arvee, we're going to the Neighbourhood Security Office!'

She grabbed his arm and began to march away in the direction of Lantana Enclave's boundary, while Diss called after their backs, 'You watch your whiskers, Miss! Or I'll have you fined for Suspicious and Unseemly Awareness of Legal Information!'

The two friends hurried along in silence for several minutes, with Ellie clutching the ant cage. Arvee was silent, thinking about the strange changes that had come over the lives of his friends in his absence. He was also worrying about how he'd manage his return journey to Paradise Villa before Mo woke up if he didn't get his bike back. It would take at least three or four times as long to walk the same distance. Ellie was too angry to speak.

When she had calmed down a bit, she said, 'It all began with the snake.' She described her moment of horror, up in the lantana bush above her home, when she saw the monstrous creature with a baby mouse in its mouth, 'I don't think it even saw me. It just put its head down again and hurried away. But I couldn't twitch a single whisker for hours afterwards.

'From the time it first appeared, the shrews began visiting our colony. They normally lived on the other side of the garden, near the kitchen. They claimed they had heard about the snake and had come to offer advice on how to prevent further attacks. It all happened so quickly. The next thing we knew, they had taken over security operations in our sector of the garden.'

The two mice were jogging along, ducking under the lower branches of the lantanas and hopping over stones, roots and knobbles of earth. 'We were just beginning to relax after the dark days of the rats in Paradise Villa and then suddenly here it was again, another kind of darkness! The snake has an awful smell and behaves strangely. There are even stories that it's deformed in some way, or it has another creature riding on its back! Oh, rumours began to fly around. No one knew what to believe. It was awful. It still is. Even three months after that first encounter, I have dreadful nightmares and wake up with my whiskers in knots!'

'How absolutely awful,' said Arvee in a quiet voice. Strong emotions were pulling him in several different directions at once. Fear, anger, confusion, and the powerful desire to set things right.

According to Ellie, since the first incident there had been a steady increase in tragedies. Young mice were at greatest risk. 'Somehow, the snake figures out when and where a baby has been left alone. Then he breaks into that home and snatches the child,' said Ellie. 'It's got so bad that everyone's terrified of going out. And yet it continues to happen: the parents are called away from home on one pretext or another and when they get back . . .' She shook her head mutely, overcome with sudden tears.

Arvee smoothed back his whiskers. 'What about the shrews? Do they suffer any . . . casualties?'

Ellie shrugged. 'According to them, it's our presence that has attracted the snake here. They claim they've had centuries of experience dealing with "h'environmental 'azards", as they put it, so they're best equipped to help us get used to our "changed circumstances" et cetera, et cetera. We've done everything we've been told to do. All movement in and out of the Enclave is severely restricted. Even news. It's very, very difficult to know what's true and what isn't. Every mouse is afraid to speak up, to share opinions, to do anything but just look after his or her own tiny patch of earth. We go about our daily business the best we can but – ' She broke off. 'Oh, look! We're nearing the Neighbourhood Security Office now. I'll have to brief you about how to behave.'

She drew Arvee closer to her and then pretended to need his help to fix the buckle on her shoes, so that her head was close to his. In this position she said, 'Please – it's of the utmost importance: be absolutely polite with the shrews. They take offence at the slightest thing! Don't say anything negative, not even "no" or "can't". Just nod your head as if you're agreeing with them and then express yourself clearly, in such a way that they can't misunderstand you or find ways to complain that you got them muddled up with your "mousy" logic. OK?'

'Understood,' said Arvee. 'I'll keep my sarcasm under my belt!'

She straightened up, appeared to test the buckle, then stepped forward. Within the next couple of seconds, they were standing outside a structure made from a number of old plastic storage boxes. It was in the shadow of the lantana bushes closest to the sandstone path and the boundary wall. Windows and doors had been cut into the boxes. At the entrance to the first one was a small signpost with a pair of big round plastic cartoon-eyes on it, of the kind whose pupils move when they're jiggled. In the context of the Neighbourhood Security Office, the eyes didn't look funny at all.

'Here we are,' said Ellie.

4

LUNCH BREAK!

Thursday Midday

Inside the first storage box was a reception desk and a huge noticeboard with pictures of mice on it. There was, of course, no writing, but the pictures were accompanied by paw prints pinned up beside them. Behind the desk, a fat shrew lolled in the depths of a vast velvet-covered beanbag, absent-mindedly picking its nose. It was hard to tell whether it was male or female.

'Please, sir,' said Ellie, hoping the shrew was male, 'I'm here to recover Snatched Property. Whom should we see?'

'Lunch break,' said the shrew, not ceasing her nasal investigation. 'And it's MADAM, thank you very much. Obviously, you're blind. Like all mice. Come back tomorrow.'

'OK,' said Ellie, 'but we've got to recover the property before – '

'Are you deaf as well as blind?' squeaked the shrew, baring her tiny sharp teeth. 'LUNCH BREAK, I said!' She made a guttural sound midway between a spit and cough. '*Khuh*. Mice. Never clean their ears.'

'Of course. But there's another matter and it can't wait either: registration for my friend here. I need to present my voucher ant and – '

The shrew slammed her paw down on the desk. 'All right,' she snarled, 'I'll say it just once more, and I'll say it loud enough for even a mosquito-brain such as yourself to understand me.' She began to struggle out of her seat in her desire to emphasize her point. 'THIS IS MY LUNCH BREAK!'

Arvee could feel a tide of anger rising up inside him. Who gave the shrews the right to be so rude and officious? Living in the garden might have taught them a few survival tactics, but it seemed to him they needed to learn some basic lessons in common decency as well.

While the shrew was still wallowing in the depths of the beanbag, Ellie said, 'I'm very sorry, madam, but the rules clearly state that urgent business can be transacted even during a lunch break. That's the rules and this *is* urgent business. Both matters. So please – could you tell me where to go?'

The shrew had to curl herself into a round ball before finally escaping the beanbag's clutches. Leaping to her paws, she whipped around now, facing Ellie directly for the first time. She was drawing in a breath, as if priming her lungs for loosing a blast of truly foul language, when she caught sight of Arvee, who'd been standing just outside her range of vision till then.

Her behaviour changed as completely as if a switch had been turned off. Stumbling back from the desk, she gave a despairing little shriek. '*Ack!* Wh-what's th-th-that THING standing next to you?'

Arvee stepped forward quickly. He'd seen this reaction before in animals who had never met an albino mouse before: unreasoning fear. It always made him feel like an ugly freak. Nevertheless, he'd learned how to take advantage of the fear. 'Oh, hello,' he said, leaning over the desk. 'It might be a good idea to pay as much attention to the blockages in your ears as to those in your nose! I distinctly heard Miss Ellie telling you that she had a FRIEND she needed to REGISTER. Well . . . I'm that FRIEND, madam! And I am, as must be obvious to someone as sharp-eyed as yourself, a mouse. Now, if you don't mind, could we get on with the matter at hand?'

'Ah-ah . . . ah – please! Your whiskers! D-d-d-on't let them touch me – ah! Ah . . . *Eek!*' And with that the distraught animal scuttled out from behind the desk and dashed through the partition that extended across the middle of the box. From the other side came the sounds of a hectic scrabbling through papers and a rummaging through drawers. A full minute later, the shrew returned, leaning backwards in an exaggerated way, as if she would much rather have been retreating from instead of entering the room. In her paws were a scrap of paper, an inking pad and a small cage. Inside the cage was an ant.

'H-here's everything you'll n-n-need for a r-r-r-registration, Miss,' said the shrew, her short whiskers trembling so much they looked blurred. 'I'm sure you know what to do: administer the oath . . . record his statement on our recorder ant and . . . and t-t-t-take his p-p-paw p-p-p-print. Then – j-j-just leave everything here on my desk, along with the voucher ant you brought with you. Confiscated properties are in the third building – access from outside. And now please! I've g-g-g-got to get on with m-m-m-my LUNCH!'

The shrew fled back through the partition, having dumped her burdens on the table.

Ellie and Arvee looked at one another and burst into silent giggles. It was so awful, it was absurd!

'Well, we'd best get on with it, then,' said Ellie when she'd recovered.

She picked up the cage with the recorder ant in it. 'Remember how you taught individual ants back in Paradise Villa to memorize messages for us?'

Arvee nodded his head. The ants, like some parrots, had the ability to record and repeat sounds. The mice in Paradise Villa had used ants as a type of communication network. Arvee had improved upon their technique of teaching messages to the little creatures so that individual ants could be made to 'play back' messages like tiny, living audio recorders.

'Well,' said Ellie, 'the shrews have taken your method one step further. They feed messages to ants, then they keep the ants captive, in cages, in their central Record Room here at the Neighbourhood Security Office – '

'Ingenious!' said Arvee, impressed in spite of himself. 'They're using living ants in the place of written records!' In his mind he could already see a research paper just waiting to be written: *Record-keeping in Pre-literate Societies.* 'But what do they feed the ants? And how do they motivate them to cooperate?' he wanted to know. His approach had been to feed the ants grains of sugar while stroking and petting them.

Ellie looked bleak. 'You're going to hate this,' she said. 'They place a tiny droplet of spider venom on the ants' antennae. That sort of paralyses them, but doesn't kill them. They're kept like that, in suspended animation, with their cages covered, until the moment when they're to be exposed to a message. Just before that moment, they're given a few crystals of honey, which perks them up. Immediately after recording the message they're taken back into the Record Room and immobilized again! The venom dulls their instincts, so they just record and play back messages as required.'

Arvee's ruby-pink eyes filled with tears. 'Oh!' he said. 'The poor little things! What a horrible, cruel thing to do – and to think it's all on account of my technique of training them!' He began tugging at his own whiskers, as if trying to pull them out by the roots. 'Oh, Ellie, Ellie! What your father said when we first met was right, after all. My ideas are all wrong for the world outside the Lab! They cause more harm than good – '

'No!' said Ellie. She caught her friend by his shoulders and shook him hard. 'Stop that! Don't take it out on yourself. There's no point. This is just one of many terrible things that have happened here and are continuing to happen. You certainly weren't responsible for all of them. And you're still our best hope for finding a way to stop all of it, because you're living outside the Enclave, free of restrictions.'

Arvee let go of his whiskers. His head drooping and in a dull whisper, he said, 'You're right, of course. Sensible, kind and clever Ellie. Come on, then. Let's get on with what we came here to do.'

5
AN EXCITING NOTE

Late Thursday Afternoon

Arvee's ride back to Paradise Villa, after getting his bike out from the Snatched Property Depot, was slow and sad. Every centimetre of the way was an effort. He was already extremely late, but he simply could not build up the energy to pedal hard.

To make matters worse, as he approached the veranda outside Mo's room, Arvee saw that his young friend was sitting on the steps, her face in her hands. Her shoulders were heaving as if she were crying. He guessed she'd woken up, found him gone and then grown frantic when she couldn't locate him anywhere inside the house.

It made him feel very guilty to see her. Mo was still a child. It wasn't right to cause her so much anxiety! He dismounted from his bike and plucked a pansy for her from a nearby flowerbed. As he wheeled his way up to her, he told himself that he must appear to be happy, for her sake.

Mo's head snapped up as she heard the sound of his small bicycle nearing. 'Oh, *Ar*-vee!' she cried. '*There* you are! Oh, you *naughty* mouse! I'm SO glad you're back!'

Arvee threw down his bike and scrambled on to the palm of her outstretched hand. He gave her the flower, then ran nimbly up her arm, until he could nestle close to her warm neck, under the curtain of her silky, sweet-smelling black hair. The happiness and love in her voice were like a tonic. He couldn't explain his troubles to her. Nor did he think she would be in a position to help or to be understanding – she didn't have the least idea of his friendships with other mice. Nevertheless, he was extremely glad to be back with her.

He spent the rest of the day being extra-attentive to Mo's needs. He sat alongside her, reading one of his own books as she did her homework. Later, after she'd had her dinner and was in bed, he changed into his pyjamas and lay on the crown of her head, as she read a passage out loud from *The Wind in the Willows*. Only when she was asleep did he hurry back up to *Mercara*.

Arvee made himself a snack for dinner. Then he went to his study to look at a packet given to him by Ellie, just before they parted company outside the Neigbourhood Security Office. She'd said, with a secretive smile on her face, 'I think you might be interested in this!' He'd been so busy socializing with Mo that he'd not had time to open the gift until now. He looked the small parcel over carefully. Then he shook it. Then he sniffed it a few times. I wonder what's inside, he thought to himself. It was completely flat and not much thicker than a bit of cardboard folded in half. Then at last he undid the wrapping paper. And his whiskers almost fell out with excitement!

Inside was a sheaf of papers, neatly cut and shaped to look like a handmade notebook. On the topmost sheet were the words 'I CAN RITE'.

Arvee was so delighted that he couldn't stop himself from dancing up and down the room. 'This is *wonderful*!' he chortled to himself. 'There I was, wondering how in the world I'd stay in touch with Ellie – and meanwhile, in my pocket, I had the answer all along! We can *write* to one another!' It was a good ten minutes before he could settle down to read what was written in the little notebook.

'RV' began the letter, 'RITING IZ NOT EASY. IT IZ MY 4TH TRI. YOUR ABCD BOOK IZ A BIG HELP. IT HAS BROT ME TO THIS POINT. BUT THAIR IZ A GRAIT DEEL THAT REMAINS FOR ME TO NO. MY SPELING FOR EXAMPUL. I HAV NOT UNDERSTUD ABOT YUSING TH LITUL MARX LIK TH COMA AND

35 🐝

FUL STOP. SO I ONLY YUS TH FUL STOP. TOON IZ ALL SO LURNING. BY THE TIM U RETURN TOON WILL HAV A PLAN FOR MAKING KON TAKT. ALL SO FOR DEE LIVER RING MESEJEZ. IT IZ VERI TIRING TO RITE. NOW I MUST STOP. YOR FREND LE.

In small letters at the very end of the last page, Ellie had written: I MISS U A LOT.

Arvee read the note over and over again. He could only imagine what a huge effort it had cost her to write even this much. 'Things have already changed since she wrote this,' he said to himself. He had got into the habit of speaking out loud whenever he was alone, because it helped overcome his loneliness when he had no one his own size to talk to. 'I wonder what Toon's system of communication is.'

Before the renovation of Paradise Villa, there were half a dozen ways in which a mouse could enter and exit the human dwelling: ancient mouse excavations, disused plumbing structures, rotting sections of wood. Though no other mice lived with Arvee in *Mercara*, he'd had a pair of friendly black beetles to keep him company. But ever since the renovation, they, like the ants, spiders, lizards, moths, cockroaches and all the other unofficial residents of the house, had to relocate. Even the woodwork of the doors and windows had been extensively repaired and refitted, and all the windows had nylon-mesh screens over them to keep mosquitoes out.

Arvee hadn't been back long enough to check whether every hole and gap had been sealed. Unlikely as it seemed that anything had been left undone, the important thing for him was to find a way of entering and leaving Paradise Villa without needing humans to open the doors. If he found nothing, then he'd have to bore a hole through the masonry himself. Arvee yawned and stretched. If he was going to design a personal tunnel to the outside world, he'd need some sleep! 'Time enough to work on it tomorrow,' he said to himself.

But he was wrong.

6

KNOCK, KNOCK! WHO'S THERE?

Friday Morning

The next day dawned as it usually did for Arvee, with Mo turning on the Japanese globe lantern over the roof of *Mercara*. He'd already done an hour of exercises and meditation by that time. He normally spent a few moments socializing with Mo before she left for school and today was no exception.

He was so busy working out a scheme for meeting Ellie that he didn't notice Mo hadn't been in her school uniform in the morning. But even if he'd noticed, he couldn't have known that she'd taken a holiday from school on account of his absence the previous day. He had no idea that for some weeks Mo and her mother had been talking about making an important change in his life. They believed it would be for his benefit. After his trip to Lantana Mouse Enclave, when they thought he was lost, they took a momentous decision on his behalf. They made phone calls and finalized arrangements. On Friday morning, they acted on their decisions.

All without breathing a word to Arvee.

At three o'clock, around the time when Mo usually came back from school, Arvee was up in his observatory. He was pleased with himself. He'd discovered that the nylon-mesh screens that covered the windows were secured by strips of Velcro attached to their edges. This meant that, as long as the window was open, all he had to do was lift up one corner of the Velcro strip, slip under it and step out on to the windowsill.

Best of all, just alongside the table on which *Mercara* was placed, there was a window that was always left open for cross-ventilation. It, like the other windows, had the nylon-mesh screen stretched across its inner frame. Arvee had already tested his mountain-climbing tackle on the screen. It wasn't exactly easy, but after a few tries he was able to throw up a grappling hook so that it caught in the mesh. He climbed up and fastened two lines of embroidery-thread rope to the screen, then fashioned a sturdy ladder for himself out of the rope.

His plan was to wait till it was night before going up. Once there, he'd slip under the Velcro strip and – out! There was a generous ledge on the other side. Using his torch, he would summon a Mantis Airline flight and fly to the neem tree. The previous year he'd learned the method of using the huge, unruly praying mantises for getting about.

All he needed now was to take the proper kit with him: rubber bands with which to strap himself into place on the mantis, mantis fees for the round-trip airfare and, of course, the gifts. He'd bought something for everyone.

'Hmm,' he said to himself. 'What exactly, I wonder, are the weight restrictions on those pesky insects?' He knew he couldn't possibly carry all the gifts he'd brought back for Ellie, Toon and the others! Still, he should be able to take a few of them on this first excursion. He'd just got his knapsack up on the work table and was busy undoing its buckles when the door from Mo's room opened.

Mo approached his table. She was carrying something in her hands.

Arvee smiled and waved at her distractedly. He was too immersed in his plans to notice that the young girl's face was lit up with excitement. She came and stood at the edge of his table, but didn't call out to him. She sometimes enjoyed just watching him go about his business, in his home. This was especially true when he was in the observatory, because the bubble of clear plastic made it easy for her to see him. As a mouse who valued his privacy, he'd found the attention intrusive in his early days at Paradise Villa. But since then he'd grown so used to Mo that he rarely noticed her when she was in what he called 'surveillance mode'.

So he continued with what he was doing until he heard a very unfamiliar sound. He didn't even identify it right away, it was so unexpected. It sounded as if Mo were rapping with her knuckles on the edge of the table. Yet from where he stood, up at the very top of his home, he could see she was doing nothing of the sort.

Then it came again, and more insistently: a knocking sound.

Arvee stood still, frowning. It sounded very much as if the rapping were coming from someone standing at his front door, using the ornamental knocker that was there for the purpose. This was most unusual! He never had guests who came to the front entrance. His friends, when they visited, used the trapdoor.

He glanced again in Mo's direction. He noticed now that his young human friend had her hand clamped to the front of her face, as if trying to stop herself from exclaiming out loud. From experience he knew this meant she was extremely excited about something. He absolutely could not understand what it was, however! Even as he stood still, puzzling over the situation, the rapping was repeated a third time.

The only explanation Arvee could think of was that Mo had a secret she wanted him to discover for himself and that she had found some way of knocking on his door without appearing to move. There was no choice but to play along with Mo's game. He called out, as if to a visitor to his home, 'Coming!'

He ran down the three short flights of stairs till he reached his hallway. Pausing only to smooth back his silvery whiskers, he flung open the front door. The next instant, in sheer shock, he almost flung it shut again!

Standing on the doorstep was a stranger.

It was a girl mouse. White, like himself.

Arranged on the top of her head she had a pile of silky blue-white curls. Her whiskers were carefully plucked and lacquered. Her nose was coloured an unnatural shade of carmine. Her eyes were blue and her eyelashes were painted black, seeming almost as long as her whiskers. She wore a tight flowery pink blouse with a short matching skirt and bright pink high heels. She carried her tail in a highly affected manner, tucked round her hips and folded over her left arm. In her hands she held a small lace handkerchief with which she was fanning herself, even though it wasn't in the least warm. A heavy, flowery scent emanated from her. Just behind her, in a neat row, were four large pink leather suitcases, all monogrammed with the letters 'QTπ'.

'Aah . . . hello!' said the stranger, in a voice which shooshed and tinkled like sparkling water poured over ice cubes. 'Dr Arvee, I presume?' Then, as Arvee continued to gape at her, she extended a dainty paw and said, 'Allow me to introduce myself. My name is Cutie Pie. I'm sorry if this comes as a bit of a shock! It was all arranged by Dr Shah, back at the Lab. He said you might be surprised, but that you'd understand as soon as you heard his name – '

At this, right on cue, Arvee swallowed and gulped. 'D-Dr Shah? From my Home Lab? *He* sent you here?'

'That's right,' said Cutie, fluttering her eyelids. 'I do hope you're going to ask me in. It's been rather a long trip, you know, and I'm just *longing* for a hot shower . . .'

Arvee was normally a very polite mouse, but his next words were rude by any standards, 'I'm sorry, but. . . but. . . *why* are you here?' he blurted out. 'Surely there's been some sort of mistake!'

Cutie was not the least bit dismayed. She smiled coyly, in a way that made her whiskers tremble appealingly. 'A mistake? Ohh, nononono!' she said. 'Quite the contrary, darling! As you can see –' she half-turned, indicating her suitcases '– I'm here to stay. I've been chosen from a long list of potential candidates to be . . . your fiancée!'

7

DANCING TO A HUMAN TUNE

Friday Afternoon

Arvee glanced up towards Mo. Her skin and eyes were glowing in the way of a would-be matchmaker. Out of a very genuine desire to provide for his happiness, imagining him to be lonely, Mo had created an all-out calamity for her pet. She had no way of knowing that he wouldn't be grateful. So for Mo's sake, Arvee knew he must pretend to go along with her plans.

He held his front door open. 'Come in,' he said to Cutie. He forced himself to smile, but inside his thoughts were whirling like autumn leaves caught up in a tornado.

'Goodness!' exclaimed Cutie as she crossed the threshold of *Mercara*. 'This is grand!' Her ears were positively twittering with excitement. 'I had no idea that scholars lived so well outside the Lab . . .'

'Urrm,' said Arvee, stepping in behind her, 'now see here, Miss Cutie, I – '

Cutie turned. 'Ooo,' she said. Her ears, eyes and whiskers were all dancing in unison now. 'Arvee, dear, don't you think you've forgotten something?' She batted her eyelashes at him and then looked meaningfully in the direction of the door. He frowned, completely puzzled. Whereupon she smiled kindly at him, as if he were a brainless little larva, and said, 'My luggage! You left it outside . . .'

Arvee shut the door. 'Ah – yes. I did that on purpose –'

Cutie's eyes opened wide. 'On purpose! But what – '

'If only you'd let me finish, I'd tell you,' said Arvee, trying to make his voice sound firm. 'I'm afraid you've been misled. There's no question of your living in my house. So it's best if your luggage stayed outside till we can sort this problem out.'

He was looking at Cutie as he said this. He had felt so sure she wouldn't be happy to hear his words that he was very surprised to notice she was smiling. Then he saw that she wasn't looking at him but over his shoulder. He turned around to see that his front door had been pushed open from outside. By Mo. One by one, she was picking up the suitcases and placing them gently inside the house! In another few moments, all four were in the hallway. Mo shut the door once more.

Cutie's expression was smug. 'Girl power!' she said, and turned smartly on her heel. 'Come on – I'm dying to see the rest of the house!'

It was a long, exhausting tour. All the way, Cutie kept up a non-stop stream of comments about the many ways in which the house could be improved. 'A bathroom on the ground floor, I think . . . a rug on the landing . . . and how about removing this lamp?'

Arvee remained aloof and silent. He didn't want to engage his guest in a long argument when he needed time to think about arrangements for his flight later that night. He was relieved when, after the tour, Cutie decided to take a nap. Arvee showed her into the guest bedroom and said he'd wake her when it was time for tea.

Up in his observatory once more, he looked over the gifts he'd brought with him: a packet of star-shaped balloons, a crazy little mechanical cricket that hopped high in the air, a folding umbrella for Ding, tiny remote-controlled cars for all his tech-minded friends . . . he wished he could take them all! He packed his backpack to full capacity, leaving out only the heaviest and bulkiest of the presents. Then he took the bag down to the broom cupboard under the stairs in order to hide it from Cutie. He didn't want her asking any nosy questions!

At three o'clock, he heard a tapping at his study window. It was Mo. She often spoke to him, thinking that he enjoyed listening to the tone of her voice. She didn't realize that he understood her speech quite well. Still smiling in that special glowing way, she said, 'I'd like to bring you and Cutie out together, to have tea with the whole family!' It gave him an absolutely icky feeling in his tummy to contemplate what lay ahead and yet, what could he do? If he pretended to be ill, Mo's mother would call in the vet. So he gave Mo a weak smile as he tapped his watch. Holding up four fingers, he said, 'Give me four minutes!'

Mo nodded, smiling. She was quite used to his sign language by now. 'I'll be back,' she said, as she left the table-room.

Hurrying up to Cutie's bedroom door, he knocked as he called out, 'Excuse me, Miss Cutie – are you awake yet? We've been invited to tea with the humans.'

Cutie opened her door. She was wearing pink silk kimono-style pyjamas. 'Mmmmm!' she said, her voice still fuzzy with sleep. 'I had a *wonderful* nap! All kinds of *delicious* dreams . . .' Her voice had a way of sliding up and down, like a yo-yo. 'And how about *you*, darling? Did *you* have a nap too?'

In the coldest possible tones, Arvee said, 'I do wish you'd stop calling me "darling" and I hope you'll hurry up. I hate to keep people waiting – '

'But it's such short *notice* . . . And I haven't even had a *shower*!' Cutie pouted. 'A girl needs at least two hours to get dressed!' Then she added in a syrupy tone that made Arvee's nerves feel like violin strings that have been tuned too tight, 'I'm sure our Mo will understand – after all, she's a girl too!'

'I very much doubt it,' snapped Arvee. 'She's perfectly punctual in all her timings.' He turned to go, without looking back at his guest. 'I'll wait for you downstairs. If you're not ready when she comes, I'll leave without you.'

Once again, however, Cutie had her way. Not only did Mo wait for the new mouse to be properly dressed, but she brought a special little basket for her pets to ride in. It was decorated with fresh flowers and furnished inside with a soft, silken cushion. She placed both mice carefully in the basket, obviously intending that they should sit side by side. Cutie was wearing a flouncy, satiny concoction, all straps and fiddly bits. Her hair was, if possible, even more curly than before and her eyelashes appeared to have grown another centimetre. She lay back on the cushion with a languorous, practised air, as if she had spent her entire life doing nothing else.

Arvee, meanwhile, was wearing his usual winter gear of blue polo neck and jeans. Next to Cutie, I probably look like a tramp, he thought, but I prefer it that way. He pretended he had no idea that the cushion was meant for sitting on. As soon as Mo had placed him inside the basket, he'd leaped on to her wrist and run nimbly up her arm, to sit on her shoulder. If Mo was taken aback, she did not say so.

The next couple of hours were an ordeal for Arvee. He knew that whatever was being done was supposedly for his benefit. Yet no one had bothered to find out what *he* really wanted. There's nothing worse, he realized, than being forced to accept an unwanted kindness. It makes an animal aware of how little he is understood by the very people who love him and whom he loves: one of the loneliest, most desolate feelings in all the world.

Arvee and Cutie were placed in the centre of the humans' dining table. Sitting round the table, staring down at them, were Mo's parents and two of Mo's girlfriends from school. Arvee's heart was pounding with indignation. He felt like a circus exhibit, yet there was *nothing* he could do! Even if he found some way later on to beg his human friend never to subject him to such a display again, for the time being, for her sake, he had to cooperate.

Meanwhile, Cutie was cavorting about like a windup toy. She fluttered her eyelashes and did pirouettes like a professional performer. It made him sick to see it. But he could tell that for all the gathered humans this was vastly more appealing than his own reserved and dignified behaviour.

The humans had already been served their tea. In the centre of the table, where Arvee and Cutie were, a mouse-sized trolley and chairs had been placed, with their own tea things. Cutie, instead of just sitting down and having her tea, insisted on pouring out a cup for Arvee.

From all round the table, cries rang out: 'How sweeeeeeeet!' and 'Aren't they the most darling pair!' and 'He looks *so* happy – almost dazed!' and 'We must have a proper wedding!' Whereupon Cutie straightened up, curtsied, blew kisses to each one of them in turn, then stood with her paw on the back of Arvee's chair, as Mo's father took out a camera and recorded the moment.

For Arvee, every word, every sound was like a laser-dart piercing his soul. From being a scholar and a scientist, he was being forced to behave like an object of idle fun, a living toy, with no individuality or dignity. Then, 'Put on some music!' rang out a voice. 'Let's see them dance!'

Mo intervened. 'Not our music, please,' she said, it's too loud for them.' She brought out a tiny music box of the kind that has a cylinder and a handle to turn it. 'Here, this should be all right.' And then, in her thoughtful and considerate way, as if she had begun to guess that the event was causing Arvee much distress, she put the music box down near him. 'Why don't you do this, Arvee? I know you enjoy it when you're on your own.'

Arvee sprang up to the task. The tune on the cylinder was Beethoven's 'Für Elise', but by cranking the handle of the music box very fast, he could make the tune sound comically racy. Cutie pranced and capered to the music. She'd brought two extra-long scarves with her. She used these now as dancing props, flinging them this way and that, causing them to wave about in graceful loops. The humans seemed to find everything she did captivating.

When he felt he'd done enough, Arvee let go of the handle of the tinkling cylinder, then rather pointedly yawned and stretched. Mo got the message right away. 'Oh, they're tired! We'd better stop.' Allowing everyone a last look to say goodbye and thank you, she packed the two mice into their little basket and took them back to the table-room.

8

FLYiNG MONSTERS

Friday Evening

Cutie dashed into *Mercara* ahead of Arvee, saying that she intended to 'fix dinner' for both of them. He told her he was perfectly capable of looking after his own meals. But she was determined to have her way and ran straight into the kitchen while Arvee shut the front door.

The next moment she shot back out into the hallway, squeaking loudly. 'MONSTERS!' she cried. *'Huge black – MONSTERS!'* Her normally very well-behaved tail was wiggling wildly and her whiskers were standing on end. 'Oh, oh, help! Here they come!' She squeaked again, sprang up in the air, narrowly missing one of the light fittings, and practically flew up the stairs towards her room.

Bounding out of the kitchen came two huge, black, shiny creatures, six legs whirring, antennae churning the air . . . but they weren't in the least interested in Cutie. 'Whee and Hum!' exclaimed Arvee. 'Oh – how nice to see you both!'

They were his two beloved pet black beetles that he'd left in the care of Ellie's cousin Toon, before going away on his long trip. 'My – you've grown, haven't you?' he laughed, as both creatures barrelled into him, pushing him so hard that he fell over with a bump! He knew it was only because they were so happy to see him. When he'd first met them, they'd been the size, relative to him, of a pair of Labradors to human beings. Now they were the size of Great Danes. 'And – oh, goodness – are those *wings* I see on your backs!'

Both beetles hummed and whistled, in the way that had earned them their names. They popped open their black shiny wing cases and pumped the delicate-looking but strong wings beneath. The slightest buzz and both beetles were airborne. It was an impressive demonstration of their newly acquired skills.

Arvee chuckled, saying, 'Really cool, gals. I guess you've become adults now!' Arvee stroked and petted them, tickling them at the base of their antennae in the way that they loved. Then he got up and led them into the kitchen. 'I bet you've still got those ravenous beetle

53

appetites, yes?' he said, as the pair bounced up and down in the air. 'Not to worry, I've got just the stuff for you. And you know what, sweeties – I'm so happy you chased that busybody house guest of mine out of here that I'm going to give you a full bowl of ice cream each!' He gave the two beetles generous helpings and then took one himself.

It was only while Whee and Hum were bent over their bowls, concentrating on their snack, that Arvee noticed a slip of something white looped round Whee's left back leg. 'What's this – a note?' he said.

It was written on a sheet of paper that had been carefully rolled up within a bit of plastic and taped round the insect's leg. When Arvee had unrolled the paper, he saw that it was a message from Toon. 'HI RV', said the note. 'AZ U CAN SEE MY RITING SKILS HAV IMPROOVD! LE SEZ SHE MET U. GRATE! NOW U MUST COM TO TH NEEM TREE. WE WILL SEND OUR MANTIS TO UR WINDOW SILL AT 11. DID U NOTICE WE UNDID THE WINDOW TAPE IN ONE PLACE? MANTIS CODE IS SHORT-SHORT-LONG-SHORT-SHORT. C YA!' Then, in a PS, Toon had added, 'BET UR HAPPY TO SEE WEE AND HUM AGAIN! THEY CANT CARRI PASSENGERS BUT THEYR GRATE WITH MESSAGES! IF U WANT TO SEND 1 BACK JUST ATACH IT LIKE I DID THEN SAY NEEM TREE VERY LOUDLY. THEYL COME RITE HERE.'

Arvee beamed. Despite all that had gone wrong, at least there were a few things going right! He wondered if Toon and Ellie were the only ones to have learned to read or whether their example had helped others to learn too. It made *such* a difference, being able to exchange notes!

'First things first,' he said to himself. 'I'll send a reply back with Whee to say I'll be there. Then I'll get myself ready to go. But what'll I do about Cutie? Worry about it later, I suppose!'

He dashed off a quick note, being careful to print in block letters, just in case Toon and the others were unable to read joined-up writing. He curled the note back into the same bit of plastic that Toon had used and reattached it to Whee's back leg.

'OK!' he said to himself, once he was done. 'Now what? Do I lead Whee out to the window? And how did she get in here anyway?' As if in answer, Whee tapped on his shoulder to make him look at her, then rose up on her back legs in the way she had when she was especially excited about something. 'OK,' said Arvee, 'so you're trying to tell me something – but what?' Whee paused delicately and then, using just the tip of one antenna, lightly tapped his mouth. 'Oh!' exclaimed Arvee. 'You're asking me to tell you where to go, now that you have a message strapped on! Clever girl! OK, Whee – to the NEEM TREE, it is, to the NEEM TREE!'

Beetles don't laugh or talk, but Whee practically did a somersault in the air as she scrambled to get herself off on her mission. *ZOOOOOOOM,* she flew, and *bump-ta-bump-ta-bump* – on a zigzagging course from the hallway and to the piano room at the back, banging into walls and corners along the way. The back window was open. 'Aha – I guess Toon must have left it ajar whenever last he was here,' said Arvee, as he scrambled after the beetle. He wanted to see where she went. Hum tagged along too, but apparently did not expect to go. Whee paused on the sill of the back window long enough to allow Arvee to catch up. Then, launching herself from there, she flew out of *Mercara*.

First she landed on the rim of the table. Then she turned her narrow head this way and that as if testing for unforeseen dangers. After all, it was still only five thirty in the evening. There was a chance that a human might come into the table-room and, catching sight of a big black beetle, try to swat it or catch it. When she was satisfied there was no danger about, she buzzed her wings and took off.

The Velcro binding of the mosquito screen was about sixty centimetres away. Landing with expert precision just above it, Whee turned herself around so that her head was now towards the ground. Tucking her long antennae under the Velcro, she bent her head and then, with the surprising agility of an insect and using her forelegs to pull herself through, she curled her whole bulk under the strip. Arvee saw the dark blot of her silhouette appear on the other side of the pale yellow screen. A moment later, she had buzzed her flight wings once again and soared away into the golden orange light of the sunset.

'My! Whee's really smart, isn't she, Hum?' said Arvee. The beetle rattled her wing cases and rose up in the air, flapping her antennae up and down. 'Bet you are too! And Toon's a real genius for sorting out our communication.' He yawned and stretched. 'Time to make ourselves a sandwich for supper before getting a little rest.'

Four hours later, Arvee woke up. The Japanese lantern that hung over *Mercara* had been switched off. A faint bluish light entered his bedroom window, suggesting that moonlight was streaming into the table-room from the garden. Faint regular creaking noises from the far corner told Arvee that Hum was fast asleep there, the hard armour-plated contours of her body expanding and contracting as she breathed.

Arvee turned on his pocket-torch and moved as noiselessly as he could manage around his room. He didn't want to risk waking Cutie. He dressed for his flight. Earlier, he'd left a note on the refrigerator for her to say that she should help herself to a snack for the night. His guess was that she must have emerged, found the note, decided to take his advice and was now safely in bed in the guest room.

He opened the door to his room and peeked out. The house was in darkness. Good! By now, Hum had woken up too and was following Arvee's footsteps closely. He hoped she wouldn't try to use her wings just now. In the close confines of the little mansion, the whirring sound they made would be quite deafening. Silently, Arvee crept out of his room and climbed down one flight of stairs. Standing on the darkened landing, he turned his sensitive ears this way and that, hoping to catch any sounds of wakefulness from the guest room. But there weren't any.

Holding his breath, he eased himself down the next flight of stairs. Soon he was standing in the hallway.

'Almost done!' he breathed in relief when he got there. 'Now to get my backpack out of the broom cupboard . . .'

He had locked the cupboard and looped the key round his neck on a string. Groping for the string now, he pulled it out from under his polo neck. He bent down and slid the key into the hole. So far so good. With a well-oiled *snick* the key turned in the lock. That was when Arvee made his mistake. Forgetting that the key was still attached to the string round his neck, he straightened up. The string snapped. The key jerked sharply, fell out of the keyhole and then on to the floor with a loud tinkle!

As the last echoes died away, Arvee heard, with a sinking heart, unmistakable rustling sounds from the room overhead. Cutie must be getting out of her bed. A few seconds later, there was a faint click, as she turned on the light in her room. Then she opened the door to her room and called, 'Arvee? Is that you? I heard a noise!' Light flooded out across the upper landing.

Quick! He had to think of something, anything, to keep her in her room! 'Hum!' hissed Arvee to the alert beetle by his side. 'You can do it! Go up –' he grabbed one of her antennae and pointed it up the stairs – 'go up and keep guard outside the guest room! Go on!' Now he thumped the insect's shiny black forewings, 'I'll manage all right on my own!'

Hum sprang up. With a tremendous racket of wings she buzzed up the stairwell. Almost instantly, there was a shriek from overhead – and the wonderful sound of the guest-room door being slammed shut again. Loud creaks told Arvee that Cutie must have jumped back into her bed, perhaps hiding under the covers! Meanwhile, Hum could be heard scraping her antennae hopefully round the edges of the guest-room door, trilling softly, like a big, friendly Great Dane puppy begging to be allowed in.

Arvee chuckled softly into his whiskers. That should keep Cutie safe for the night, he thought. He hoisted his knapsack on to his back, hooked his torch on to his belt and wrapped a long length of rope round his waist. 'Time to go!' he whispered.

9

LOOK OUT BELOW!

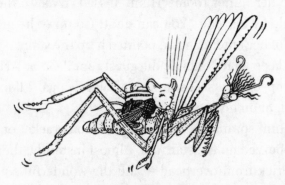

Late Friday Night

Arvee's Mantis Airline flight took less than ten minutes to reach the neem tree in the centre of the garden. Two rows of glow-worms were blinking along the third branch from the top of the tall tree to guide the flight in for a landing. As the giant insect touched down with its characteristic bump, almost unseating the passenger straddled across her ample abdomen, a cheer rang out from somewhere near the trunk of the huge tree. 'He's here, he's here!' cried at least a dozen mouse voices, among which Arvee felt sure he recognized Toon's.

What a wonderful delight it was to be back with his friends! Arvee could feel the tension of the past couple of days drop away from him like a sweaty tracksuit. 'Hello, hello!' he responded, and a moment later he was engulfed in hugs and back-thumps and then more hugs. In less time than it took to say, 'Whiskers!' he was swept up and carried into a dark aperture in the trunk of the tree.

A heavy black cloth had been drawn across the mouth of a long deep hole in the tree. The moment the mice were on the other side of the curtain, Arvee saw glow-worm lights dimpling the inner darkness, illuminating a tall interior space. It was heavily grooved and rutted with the tree's internal architecture, but also criss-crossed with ropes, light scaffolding, narrow platforms and landings leading into irregularly shaped bumps and bobbles.

As Arvee would discover later, almost two dozen mice lived here. Most were from the days of the Ratland Rebellion, but there were new recruits too. The bumps were individual rooms, made out of straw and mud. The central meeting place was a long cylinder of nylon webbing, of the kind that is sometimes used for packing wine bottles. The webbing had been reinforced with toothpicks and drinking straws to give it shape, and it hung down through the centre of the space. A number of beautifully crocheted slings provided ample seating within the webbing. It was like a vertical nest of small hammocks into which the mice could climb whenever they needed to discuss something. The nylon mesh was

61

elastic enough for mice to enter and exit the structure at any point, reaching for one of the hanging rope ladders to swing away whenever they desired.

'Welcome to our new home, Arvee!' said Zero, smiling broadly. She was looking much the same as when he had last seen her, wearing her camouflage overalls and a cap on her head. When at last the first wave of greetings was over, she said, 'We call this the Web Room – or just the Web for short – and I'm sure I speak for every single mouse here when I say how glad and relieved we are to see you!'

'Hear, hear!' said many voices, and, 'Speech! Speech!'

'Yes,' said Toon, smiling warmly. 'You're the traveller! Tell us everything – but mind, we'll have to pause for a snack at least once every hour!'

Everyone laughed.

For Arvee, looking up and around, it felt as if he were in a particularly sweet dream. 'You can't imagine,' he began, 'how often I've thought of this moment – of how I would once more be among you all, and how I would bring all the sights and sounds of my trip here to share with you.' He patted the backpack on his back. 'Of how I would unpack my gifts one by one, neatly and in the correct order! But now that I'm actually here among you, I realize that all I've experienced in these past few months is nothing compared with the gladness and happiness of being with all of you, my friends . . .' His voice was quite thick with emotion, 'I'm – well, I'm very, very glad to be back!'

Applause and cheers rang out.

'And, as I'm sure you've already heard,' said Toon, 'we've even managed to find ourselves in serious trouble once again!'

'Too right, Toon,' said Zero softly. 'We mice just can't look after ourselves.'

The mood in the Web sobered down at once. 'It's been quite dreadful,' said a voice. Arvee looked around and saw it was Horse. She was a stocky mouse, tall and strong, with a pleasant face. 'Just when we thought all our problems were over, a completely new and horrible kind of trouble appeared to take its place . . . But, sir, if you don't mind my saying so, just seeing you here with us again gives us hope – or me at least – that now we've got a real chance of setting things right.'

There was another round of cheers, but more muted this time.

'Thanks!' said Arvee, taking a deep breath. 'Well, here I am, and always at your service!'

'There are a number of mice you've not met before, Arvee,' said Zero. She called them forward by name. 'That's Bizzy and Cocky. Next to them, Whizzbang and Spud – twins, as might be obvious – followed by Squeak and Bubble. Sparx and Crax are out on scout duty. They were on the branch when you arrived.'

As each mouse was introduced, she or he swung forward on a length of rope and waved to Arvee. The twins swung simultaneously from opposite sides of the Web, exchanging ropes in mid-air like trapeze artistes at a circus. The remaining mice, Feather, Happy, Heavy, Lucky and Willing, were friends from the pre-Flood days.

Arvee smiled and waved. When all the introductions were over, he said, 'Where's Ellie? I was *so* hoping she'd be here before I arrived!'

'We're expecting her,' said Toon. He kept looking up towards the entrance. 'We exchanged notes earlier in the day, through Hum. The scouts are on the lookout – ah, there's the signal.'

Glancing up, Arvee saw a pinpoint of light near the curtain across the entrance.

'Come on, let's go!'

Along with Toon and Bubble, Arvee scrambled up and out on to the landing branch of the tree. He still had his backpack on his back, which made him a little more awkward and clumsy than he would have been without it. With all the excitement of meeting his friends again, he'd not had time to take it off.

The moment the three mice were out along the landing branch Arvee knew something was wrong. Sparx, who had gripped his hand while helping him out, looked tense. 'Crax is at the end of this branch,' he whispered to Arvee. 'He says he sees her, but. . .'

Arvee's heart missed a beat.

'Come on!' hissed Toon. 'To the end of the branch. We'll see more from there.'

'I'll stay here,' Bubble whispered. 'Got to guard the entrance.'

Arvee, Toon and Sparx scampered forward. The branch was broad where it joined the tree. Its bark was deeply grooved, as if someone had deliberately raked it with forks to create a texture. Further away from the trunk, however, the branch grew smoother and narrower. The mice moved slowly now, single file. Finally they reached the end of the landing branch.

'Crax is out at the end of that smaller branch above us,' whispered Toon. 'If you look there, you'll see him hanging head-downward on one of the leaf clusters.'

Several branchlets snaked away on either side of the main branch. The one that Toon indicated was above and to the right. It ended, as did the others, in graceful clusters of leaves. Each stem bore about fourteen clusters, the leaves shaped a bit like arrowheads, curved and serrated, pointing back towards the trunk of the tree. By straining his eyes, Arvee could just about make out a slight thickening towards the very end of one of the clusters. 'Goodness!' he said, under his breath. 'Isn't that rather dangerous?'

'The shape of the leaflets prevents him from slipping off,' Sparx explained. 'Shh – if we move forward, along this branch, we can position ourselves directly under him. He'll tell us what he can see.'

Arvee breathed in deeply. The scent of the neem tree's leaves was tart and bitter but in a pleasant way. He strained to catch whatever he could of the conversation taking place between Sparx and Crax.

'She's moving fast,' Crax was saying. 'She might just make it.'

'All right,' said Sparx. 'What about the . . . other thing? Is it still there?'

'Yep,' said Crax. He sounded grim. 'It's the snake all right. No doubt about it. It started out from where that sandstone path ends and was coming towards the tree. We've got to hope it doesn't know she's there.' Arvee's ears and tail went cold. With one part of his mind he noticed this interesting effect: the coldness resulted from all the blood in his body draining from his extremities into his muscles and brain, as he braced himself for possible action. The other part of his mind squeaked in panic to hear what sounded like a terrible situation unfolding beneath him.

Sparx asked, 'Any way that we can warn her off?'

Crax paused before saying, 'Uh-oh! The snake's stopped.'

Arvee turned to Toon. 'How does Crax know it's Ellie down there?'

'He was watching for her along the route she normally takes. We mice have always got to take precautions, as you know. So we follow certain predictable routes.'

'But why isn't she on a mantis?' Arvee wanted to know, 'It's quite a distance and with unknown lurking terrors . . .' His voice trailed away. It was certainly foolhardy for her to have attempted such a journey when there was a snake loose in the garden!

'Well,' whispered Toon, 'it's either that or not coming at all. A Mantis Airline flight can't land inside Lantana Enclave because of the . . . well, the restrictions. Till last week it was possible for us – the Neem Tree Gang we're called – to visit. But then, abruptly, our permits were cancelled. No reasons given. Since then Whee and Hum have been our sole means of contact.'

'What about the ants? Hasn't the ant line been reestablished?'

'No,' said Toon. 'Ever since the shrews began misusing the ants as "recorders" the messenger service collapsed.'

There was a sharp exclamation from Crax. 'Blistering beetle-dung! The snake's turning – it must have spotted her!'

Arvee swallowed hard.

Just then there was another sharp exclamation, this time from Sparx.

'What? What?' hissed Arvee and Toon simultaneously.

'Look!' said Sparx. 'Look – you can watch too, if you stare hard between this cluster of leaves on the right – she's still on course and moving fast. But the snake's definitely aiming towards her now . . .'

Arvee could bear the tension no longer. He jumped up and ran further along the branch that he, Toon and Sparx were on. Crouching, he headed towards the leaf clusters at the end. Grabbing hold of the stem of one of the clusters, he threw himself stomach-down on to it, wriggling forward at the same time. The long springy stem immediately bent under his weight, so that he was automatically pitched forward in a head-down position just like Crax in the branch above. Simultaneously, his heavy backpack swung over his head and almost off his shoulders.

The whole expanse of the garden came into view, seen from a great height. By the cold blue light of the moon, the smooth grass looked like a vast grey velvet field, bordered by flowerbeds, potted plants and the looming dark shapes of the trees.

On this field, as clearly as if an invisible hand were drawing an invisible pencil across it, was a ripple of movement. Something small was moving through the grass, coming towards the tree from the direction of the Lantana Enclave. Moving at right angles towards it, from the direction of the red sandstone path, was a second ripple. It was long and sinuous, with a peculiar lump near its front end. It was moving quite slowly towards the first ripple, as if savouring the thrill of the hunt. As if it had all the time in the world.

And meanwhile, on the surface of the grey-white expanse, flickered the shadow of an owl.

10

LOOK OUT ABOVE!

Friday Midnight

One moment Arvee was dangling upside-down in space, and the next, the stem on which he was lying snapped and fell away. He fell with it, spinning through the empty air, his body automatically curled up, assuming the position of least air resistance.

The only thought in his mind was: How bizarre – I believe I'm going to fall directly on to that snake! The stars and the moon were spinning around and around like a lighted carousel, the wind was whistling in his ears, as he tumbled over and over until – *BUMP!* – Arvee hit something in mid-air and –

WHOOSH! – with a flash of pale feathers, the startled owl swerved away.

Oops! thought Arvee. That was a close call –

In the very next instant – *THUMP!* – he hit something beneath him.

'OOOF!' exclaimed a loud hoarse voice.

An enormous force whipped under and away from Arvee, flinging him sideways.

'YOWW-OWWW-WWW!' yelled the hoarse voice, then continued in a language that Arvee recognized but did not understand.

The words belonged to the sibilant language of snakes, yet the speaker was not a snake. An argument was apparently in progress. The hoarse voice, shouting and cursing, was answered by another voice, presumably belonging to the serpent, protesting and complaining. But both voices were receding into the distance, going back towards the sandstone path.

Arvee tumbled over a couple of times before coming to a rest. Then everything went blank for a few seconds. When his senses returned, he was lying in tall grass under the cluster of neem leaves that had got detached at the time of his fall. He appeared to be alone. He lay still, collecting his wits. There were traces of a strong, unpleasant odour lingering in the air, over and above the scent of the neem-tree leaves. A smell he couldn't identify and had never encountered before. His mind was humming like a top, his whiskers were trembling and his heart was hammering.

He took in a deep, steadying breath. The rich earth-scented air had an immediately calming effect. The chirping buzz of thousands of night insects thrummed in his ears. In another few moments, he felt curiously relaxed. This is what it feels like to be glad to be alive, he thought to himself. How odd that we've got to have a brush with danger to be reminded of it!

Then, just as he was starting to tell himself that it would be quite pleasant to spend the rest of his entire life lying in the grass, breathing quietly and listening to insects, he felt someone's soft paw on his shoulder.

'Ellie!' he cried, leaping up. 'Are you OK?'

'Oh, my goodness, Arvee,' she gasped. 'The cobra – I thought you must have fallen straight into its mouth!'

'Who cares about cobras!' Arvee enveloped her in a big hug. 'I'm just so pleased you're in one piece!'

'Me too!' said Ellie, then giggled as she corrected herself. 'I mean, I'm glad *you're* in one piece!'

'Whee-hoo!' said Arvee, laughing delightedly. He felt so happy, he was almost fizzing. 'I don't know why, but I feel like a cola that's just been opened! As if I've been bottled up for days – for months – '

'Hey, come on, you two!' It was Toon's voice. He appeared to be bouncing in the air directly above their heads. 'There'll be time enough for mushy stuff later.' He

71

unclipped his bungee cord as he set himself down. 'Or had you entirely forgotten that it's dangerous for little mice to be out in the open? Quickly, now – this way! The grass will give us some cover, but we've got to cross a patch of bare earth before we get to the tree's trunk.'

'Toon!' exclaimed Arvee. He looked up, as if half-expecting more mice to follow. 'How did you get here?'

Toon grinned at Arvee's surprise. 'It's called bungee-jumping, Arvee, and let me assure you, it's a good deal safer than leaping off branches, assaulting owls and scaring off snakes!'

'Ooo!' exclaimed Ellie. 'Don't talk about it, please! It makes me sick to even imagine what might have happened – '

'And still *could* happen,' Toon reminded them. 'We're very exposed here on the ground – come on! Follow me.'

The three friends scampered towards the tree. There was a firefly to mark the spot where there was a knothole in the bark. Entering the hole, Toon plugged it securely with a bit of cork. Then the mice climbed all the way up until they were back with the rest of the Neem Tree Gang in the Web Room. Once Arvee, Toon and Ellie had been joyfully welcomed back, Zero called for silence.

'Friends!' she said. 'Wonderful as it is to be united and safe once more, we mustn't allow ourselves to forget the shadow that hangs over us all. Tonight's encounter was only the first instalment, the first time the snake has approached our tree. There will surely be another. Tonight we had a lucky break . . .' She paused to smile in Arvee's direction, before her expression darkened again. 'But we'll need more than luck if we want to remain where we are. Unlike in the Lantana Enclave, here in the neem tree we have no protection except vigilance – and even that, against a cobra. . .' She shook her head.

The atmosphere was thick with foreboding.

Crax spoke up. 'Well, it's a strange thing. You know how the rumours, all along, have suggested that the snake was something worse than just a snake? That it was a monster of some kind? Well, tonight, for the first time, I saw for myself that there was something odd about it.'

'We all saw it,' said Sparx, 'all three of us up in the tree. It's not an ordinary cobra, whatever else it is. It looked sort of . . . misshapen. We have no idea why or how. When it moved sideways towards Ellie, we saw more clearly that there was something definitely peculiar about its neck. Not near the head but lower down. And *after* Arvee fell on it, well! That was the most peculiar of all. I mean, it was completely lopsided.'

'Yes!' said Arvee. 'I can confirm a part of this.' He repeated what he'd heard and felt at the time he fell, in particular the two voices. 'One belonged to the snake. But the other. . .' He smoothed back his whiskers. 'A hoarse, gruff voice. Talking in snake-speak, but with a strong mammalian accent.' He shrugged. 'I have no explanation for it.'

Zero took centre-Web once more. 'My fellow mice! I'm sure each one of you knows just how deadly a threat any kind of snake is to us, monstrous or normal. Let us remind ourselves: snakes can climb trees; snakes can dig down into holes; snakes can batter down our small defences. As long as it remains in the neighbourhood, we will be at risk.

'And there's another point. This creature's appearance isn't the only strange thing about it. There's its behaviour too.' The silence in the Web Room was intense. 'The shrews say they've also suffered casualties from the snake, for which reason they're keen to discourage its presence in the garden. However, when we of the Neem Tree Gang spoke to other witnesses in the garden – the garden lizards, the squirrels, even some bats – they all said the same thing: there was one snake-related shrew death right in the beginning, in February. Then another one about a month ago. We mice, however, are raided almost every week.

'Now, that's very odd. Snakes don't discriminate between prey. One warm-blooded mammal is exactly the same to them as any other. They neither see nor taste any differences between us. This leads me to the next strange thing. It's to do with the way reptiles eat. They're not like us mammals. They don't need to eat as often as we do. Usually, if they've had a good meal, they don't need to eat again for quite a long time. Yet this cobra, as we know, has been coming out on weekly hunting expeditions.

'For both these reasons, it's clear to me that something beyond ordinary hunger is driving this beast. Something that we don't understand.'

Zero paused a long time before continuing. 'Then there's the final strangeness: from the time of the first attack onward, the shrews' campaign of fear and the loss of freedoms to the residents of the Lantana Enclave have been at least as frightening as the snake's raids. Our move to the neem tree grew out of our desire to live in freedom. Yet, being forced to live away from our families and friends is itself a loss of freedom. We can neither help them nor, it seems now, help ourselves any more. The snake has finally found us too.

'I've tried very hard to understand what the connection is between the attacks, the shrews and our loss of freedoms. I can't work it out and I don't know what we can do about it. All I can tell you for sure is that there *is* a connection.'

As Zero spoke, the atmosphere in the Web had grown progressively more sombre. Now, as she neared the end of her speech, it was as if a heavy weight were pressing down into the friendly space of the tree. 'You have all looked towards me as your leader. But in the past weeks, I haven't felt as if I had the will or the ideas to lead so much as a broken twig!'

She glanced once more towards Arvee. 'Your return to our midst has been the most positive thing that has happened in weeks, Arvee! Yet I think I speak for all of us here in the neem tree when I tell you that I do not expect you to shoulder our burdens for us. What we're facing may be beyond all our powers, yours included. None of us will think the worse of you if you decide you'd rather not share a fate that isn't, after all, yours to suffer.'

A low murmur of assent passed among the mice. Every eye was turned towards Arvee. He was seated close to where Zero stood, approximately in the middle of the Web. Ellie was opposite him, on the other side. It was a narrow space, so he could see her quite clearly. There was a tiny smile flickering in and out of her whiskers. He guessed she knew perfectly well what he was about to say.

Zero invited Arvee to join her in the middle of the Web, but he shook his head, 'I'll speak from where I am, Zero, and I have four things to say. One is that, as far as I'm concerned, you've always been the leader of this gang – and I wouldn't want to take your place at the centre of the Web, not even for a short while – not even if you ordered me to do it!' He smiled as he said this. There was an immediate scattering of chuckles and applause.

'The second thing is, I won't accept, even if you begged me with folded ears, the idea of abandoning you. Neither in the neem tree nor in the Lantana Enclave. Friends, the fact is, ever since I first came in contact with all of you, back there in the dark days of Ratland, I've believed that your fate *is* my fate – '

For a few moments, he couldn't continue because a tidal wave of applause, whistles and cheers from all the gathered mice engulfed him. He waited till it had passed. Then he said, in an altogether more serious tone of voice, 'That is not to say I disagree with Zero's estimation of the situation. The problems facing us are serious, complex and mysterious.' Then he paused. 'But for the time being, against the snake, I have a simple solution to offer.'

A collective gasp went up from all the listening mice. A few excited little voices called out, 'Oo! Isn't he wonderful! Tell us! Tell us!'

Arvee smiled as he held up his paw for silence. 'Patience, team! This brings me to the fourth thing I need to say.' He stood up here. 'Time is not on our side. I must get back to my home or else my human friends will come looking for me. Once I'm there I won't be able to return till after darkness has fallen and I'm betting our snake visitor will come again tomorrow night. So here's what I suggest: Ellie and Toon should fly back with me now and, between the three of us, we'll sort out the details. By nightfall, I promise you, we'll have a plan in place, and I'll finally be able to distribute these gifts!' He pointed to his backpack.

Another cheer went up from the mice. Arvee looked at Ellie and Toon. 'Assuming that's OK with you, I mean. And you too, Zero.'

Zero smiled as she said, 'Arvee, just as you've told us that our fate is your fate, I can tell you that our resources are your resources – including ourselves!' With many warm hugs and goodbyes, the three mice were escorted up to the landing branch. Three Mantis Airline flights were summoned.

'Come back soon,' said Zero to Arvee as he boarded his insect.

'In a twinkling,' he promised.

11

HOUSE-MOUSE HERO

Early Saturday Morning

Ellie and Toon both reached the window ledge before Arvee. His mantis, Madonna, landed with such a thump that he fell right off. 'Had a nice nap, eh, Mr Mouse?' she bawled down at him, as he picked himself up. Her small triangular head with its huge glittering eyes towered high in the air above him. She was at least fifteen centimetres long, with the characteristic elongated thorax and long, dangerous-looking forearms of her species. 'C'mon, gimme my fee. We working gals just gotta keep flying or we drop dead of sheer boredom!'

Arvee paid up the three raisins he'd brought along as flight charges, then Madonna pumped her four great wings and leaped into the air with a tremendous whirring commotion. 'Seeeeeeeeee yaaaaaaaaaaaah!' she screamed, as she wheeled about and vanished into the night.

Arvee brushed back his whiskers and smiled shamefacedly at his two friends. 'Sorry! I can't imagine what there is about these flights that makes me sleep.'

'They're obviously much too safe,' teased Ellie, 'for someone who's grown accustomed to falling out of trees!'

'Very funny!' said Arvee, wiggling his whiskers at her. 'I'll remember that remark the next time you're being chased by cobras!'

'By the way, Arvee,' said Toon. 'While we've been waiting out here on the ledge, I noticed a strange thing.' He jerked his thumb towards the window. 'My eyes might be deceiving me, but I thought I saw someone in *Mercara*, standing at the guest-room window.' He stopped. 'What's the matter, Arvee? You look like you've got your tail caught in the door!'

'Fried whiskers!' gasped Arvee. 'Great boiling scarabs! What a catastrophe!' His friends stared in amazement. They had never heard him use such language before. He was clutching his ears, as if he might at any moment tear them both off. 'I completely forgot about. . . about – '

'Cutie,' said Cutie, wriggling out from under the mosquito mesh.

Arvee almost fell off the window ledge in dismay.

'Yes, you certainly *did* forget about Cutie,' she said, pushing herself into the space between Arvee and Toon.

She was wearing something simple for a change, a white T-shirt and a pair of shorts. But her hair was piled up in huge bouncy curls, and her nose and eyes were glittering in the moonlight. 'Huh! Did you think you'd keep me imprisoned for ever with one stupid beetle outside my door? Did you think I couldn't open a window sash, jump down one floor to the tabletop and up the rope ladder you left there so conveniently to this idiotic, boring windowsill? Well, think again, Dr Vagabond Arvee! Just because I curl my hair and wear the latest fashions doesn't mean I have dandelion seeds in my skull! I was raised in a Laboratory, just like you! I have brains and intelligence, just like you – so don't you ever –' she leaned towards him, waggling one of her long, painted claws at his nose '– *ever* take me for granted again!'

'Uh, excuse me,' said Toon. He moved around to where she could see him. 'I think I can explain everything. We've not met.' He held out his paw to her. 'My name's Toon and this is my cousin, Ellie. I'm sorry if this comes as a surprise to you, but we're friends of Arvee's.'

Cutie turned at Toon's voice. She stared at him as he spoke, but she didn't take his paw. Instead she edged backwards away from him. Her nose was twisted sideways and her ears were turned down in exaggerated scorn. 'Yes! Just as I thought. You're not even one of us – you're just a common, dirty, uneducated HOUSE MOUSE!' She whipped around to Arvee. 'So *this* is what you do when you're playing hooky from your human!'

Arvee finally found his voice. 'Cutie –' he began.

But she cut him off. 'I've spent the whole of the night worrying about what had happened to you – wondering whether I should go and wake up our dear, sweet, *trusting* human – whether I should come after you myself – except of course I had no idea where to go or how to get down from this ledge. And all the while . . . you've been running around with a gang of mud-coloured ruffians –'

'Don't you dare describe them like that!' said Arvee, taking a step forward. He was so angry that he found it hard to speak. 'They're my best friends –'

'I'll describe them however I wish!' raged Cutie. Her voice, no longer a soft, seductive murmur, sounded more like a cicada shrieking at top volume. 'Just you wait till I tell our Mo about what you do when she's not looking! You'll see how she deals with your fungus-breath, jungle-bum companions –'

Arvee couldn't help himself. Reaching out, he gave one of Cutie's curls a good hard yank. To his complete shock, the whole mass of bluish-white hair came off in his paw. It was a wig! At the same instant, Cutie sprang back, forgetting that she was standing on a narrow ledge.

'YOW!' she squeaked in terror, as she fell backwards through the empty air.

'Oh, no!' cried Ellie. 'Quick – Toon!'

But he hadn't needed any urging. 'Coming!' he called down to Cutie. He took a moment to attach his bungee cord to a knob on the windowsill, then vaulted over the edge. 'Never fear, House Mouse Toon is here!'

'No! No!' yelled Arvee, waving his arms, but it was too late. Toon had already jumped. 'Be careful!'

'Don't worry,' said Ellie, 'Toon knows how to land safely from a height.'

'Oooh!' said Arvee, looking very fierce. 'I can't tell you how mad I am! How *dare* she talk like that – a vain, pampered mouse like her, saying such things about the dearest, bravest, most interesting friends I've ever had. Why, I could almost. . .' He didn't continue, but the way his paws were twisting the wig made it clear enough what he meant.

'Oh, come on, Arvee,' said Ellie. 'She's just not met any of us before.'

'Her rudeness isn't the only problem,' Arvee muttered. 'It's what she might say to Mo. It's hard enough fighting off serpents and shrews without having to deal with humans and their restrictions as well.'

'I thought your human didn't understand mouse-speak?'

'Cutie's pretty good at making herself understood with sign language. I guess the reason I forgot about her was that life in *Mercara* has been so awful since she came that I'd basically blanked her out of my mind.' Arvee shuddered, remembering the 'dance' session in the human dining room. 'We're about as different as a cricket is from a mosquito.'

Ellie laughed. 'Give her time, Arvee! She'll be OK, once we can explain things to her. If she's as intelligent as you are, like she says, then . . . maybe we can use her skills and expertise too. Maybe she's just not had time to know how to use her potential outside a laboratory.'

Arvee didn't look optimistic. 'I hope you're right. Because it's almost –' he looked at his watch '– oh dear! An hour from now, Mo will be waking up! We've *got* to find some way of stopping Cutie from telling tales – and we need a bite to eat – and where are those two anyway?' He peered over the side of the window ledge. It was much too dark to see anything except a general murk. 'I'm so hungry I could eat a roomful of popcorn.'

'Tell you what?' Ellie said, tugging on Arvee's tail. 'Let's get back into the house.'

'But shouldn't we wait here to help them up?' Arvee wanted to know. 'Cutie can be unpredictable and they might need assistance . . .'

Ellie shook her head. 'Toon's spent his whole young life finding a dozen different ways to scale up and down walls. Frankly, right now I'm rather more interested in that popcorn you mentioned . . .'

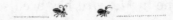

Ellie and Arvee were given an ecstatic wing-buzz welcome by Whee and Hum. They all went into the kitchen. While Ellie put out bowls of bread scraps in milk for the beetles, Arvee got out a packet of corn kernels. He roasted them individually on a paraffin-candle flame. As the kernels popped, he handed the big white puffs to Ellie for spreading butter and Nutella. Then they ate the still-warm corn with butter melting into their whiskers and sweet, nutty chocolate dripping off their noses.

Arvee explained that Cutie had been brought in from Arvee's Home Laboratory as his fiancée. 'Mo and her parents don't realize that I already have Someone Important in my life,' he said, looking meaningfully in Ellie's direction. She smiled and twiddled her nose at him. 'Cutie thinks she's engaged to me. But she's been so rude to you, I don't think I can speak to her politely ever again! Or explain how things really are.'

'Don't be so judgemental, Arvee,' said Ellie. 'She's a very attractive mouse who came here with perfectly normal hopes and dreams. It'll be tough for her to accept that they're not going to be realized.' She shrugged. 'And . . . maybe you'll change your mind too, after she's been here for a while –'

'Never!' cried Arvee, leaping to his feet.

'OK, OK,' laughed Ellie, 'don't get your whiskers in a twist! But you take my point? She needs kindness, understanding and time.'

Some fifteen minutes later, there was a scraping at the window of the piano room.

In walked Toon, with a very subdued-looking Cutie in tow. Her mascara had streaked down her cheeks.

Her nose no longer looked like a lacquered cherry. Her T-shirt was torn in a couple of places. She was covered in dust and one of her sandals was missing.

She sat meek and silent as Arvee set out a huge stack of crisp cornflakes in the centre of the table, with a choice of at least five different sauces to dip them into – tomato, mayonnaise, mango chutney, barbecue and bean-curry purée.

Ellie took pity on Cutie and said, 'You'd feel a lot better if you had something to eat, you know.'

But the other mouse shook her head, not looking up. The only thing she accepted was a mug of hot chocolate, with an almost inaudible, 'Thank you.'

When the other three had had their fill, Arvee looked up at the clock on the kitchen wall. 'Time's moving along, team!' he said. 'We'll have to decide which room's the best place for you two to hide in, Ellie and Toon. Now, Cutie . . .' He tried to give her his most serious expression, 'I'd be really grateful if you didn't discuss anything with Mo until I've had time to give you a little background about what's going on here. After that, if you still want to tell tales on me – well – we'll deal with that crisis when we get to it!'

Cutie stood up. Her ears were quivering and the tip of her tail was curled tight round her right ankle, in the attitude of a very young, defenceless baby mouse. She still couldn't look anyone in the eye. In a low voice she said, 'Don't worry – I won't make trouble for any of you.

I'll just stay out of your way and – and do whatever I'm told . . .' Stifling a sob, she stumbled out of the room.

'Goodness,' exclaimed Ellie, the moment Cutie was gone. 'She's a changed mouse!' She looked over at Toon with narrowed eyes. 'I wonder if a certain Master Toon had something to do with it?'

'Oh,' said Toon, as he scratched the untidy bush of his whiskers, 'I just taught her an old trick of mine about climbing walls, using a couple of friendly snails and . . . a whole bunch of raw, unpeeled nerves.' He chuckled. 'She screamed so much I thought the whole garden would wake up.'

'Oh, Toon,' said Ellie, 'that was mean! An owl might have been alerted and come after her while she was climbing and . . .' She stared at her cousin, her mouth agape. 'You don't mean it *did* happen?'

'You bet,' said Toon, smiling lazily. 'Bound to, what with the bright moonlight and all. But I was prepared for it, see? I'd climbed up ahead and was sitting on the sill. Saw the hooter zooming in from a long way off. Got out my catapult and bonked it in the eye before our glamorous friend became a gourmet snack! It had an excellent effect on her climbing skills, I can tell you. She was up the wall and over the windowsill in two blinks of a firefly!'

'Oh, you bad mouse!' said Ellie, laughing as she lightly cuffed Toon's ears.

12

ACTION MOUSE!

Saturday Morning

Arvee took a quick nap before getting up in time to spend half an hour with Mo. He was relieved when Cutie didn't appear. Once his human friend had left for her Saturday dance class, he hurried back to *Mercara*. 'Here I am again!' he said to Toon and Ellie, who were lying low in the dining room. 'Any news?'

A couple of messages had already come through from Zero, Toon told him. 'There was a raid on Lantana Enclave last night. The snake must have gone there after visiting us. The shrews are in a frenzy. They're convinced we mice are inviting the snake's attention. They're stringing up recorder ants from every tree and bush – recording goodness-knows-what and for no-one-knows-whom.' He shrugged perplexedly. 'It's as if the whole place has gone completely mad.'

Arvee nodded. 'We need to move quickly. We've got to be ready with a plan for dealing with the snake in case he returns tonight.'

'What about Cutie?' asked Ellie. 'Shouldn't we include her in our discussions?'

'I don't think so,' said Arvee. 'She was so rude to you both. I'm not ready to forgive her for that.'

'Arvee, it bothers you more than it does us,' said Ellie. 'It was only her second day out of the Lab. Who knows? – maybe you'd have been the same, if you'd not been alone for a couple of weeks before you met us.'

'No way!' said Arvee. 'I'd never even heard of . . . of mice outside the Lab –'

'So, that just means she's more aware of the wider world than you were! After all, we treated *you* rudely when we first met, remember? My father didn't even want us to be friends,' said Ellie. 'I think you're being a little unfair.'

'Maybe so,' said Arvee, 'but even apart from her views and her remarks, I find her annoying. I mean, she wears *blue contact lenses*, for goodness' sake, to cover up her pink eyes! It's like she's always putting on a show, for some invisible camera.'

'Well, she came down while you were away,' said Ellie. 'I was in the breakfast nook, so she didn't see me until she'd already started making a cornflake sandwich for herself. She almost ran right out again when she saw me, but I invited her to sit with me.' Ellie looked thoughtful. 'We had quite an interesting chat. . .'

'Really?' said Arvee, in the tone of someone who isn't prepared to believe what he hears.

'She's a lot smarter than you think she is,' said Ellie. 'Did you know, for instance, that she can use a computer and is fluent in a dozen languages – including Ancient Fruit Bat?'

Arvee clicked his tongue with impatience and said, 'Every Lab mouse uses computers and learns foreign languages! It's nothing special.'

'It is for me,' said Ellie, setting her ears back in the determined way she had when she wanted to stress her point. 'Especially considering that I'm barely literate in even one language!'

Toon had been drumming his claws on the table for several minutes. He cut in now. 'Listen up, team! Can't we save the character analysis for later?'

'Right you are!' said Arvee, smoothing back his whiskers. 'Back to business. The way I see it, there are three levels of challenge ahead: first, we have to ensure once and for all that the neem tree remains a safe haven or else we'll be too demoralized to resist attacks anywhere else. Second, we have to confront the shrews and break their hold over us. And third, of course, we have to make the whole of Lantana Enclave safe from the snake! Agreed so far?'

The other two nodded, their eyes bright.

'The first part is the easiest,' said Arvee. 'It came to me in a flash last night, while Zero was talking about the danger to us from snakes.'

When he'd outlined his scheme in a few words, Toon grinned. 'Oh, yes! That'll work. We've got loads of that stuff saved from what the construction workers left behind. It's all stored safely inside the tree.'

'But it'll take time to set it up,' said Ellie. 'We'd best go now, so that it'll be in place before nightfall.'

'I agree,' said Arvee, 'except it's daylight. Won't it be difficult to get from here to the neem tree without being pounced on by something or the other?'

'Oh, *Ar-vee!*' exclaimed Ellie, once she got over laughing. 'No one notices *us*! That's one of the perks of being *ordinary house mice*,' she said, deliberately teasing him. 'Even Alphonso the cat, of whom we were all so afraid in the Ratland days, doesn't pay attention to us any more! In fact, he runs in the opposite direction when he sees us in the garden.'

Arvee blushed till his nose matched his pink eyes. 'Oh, all right, then!' he said. 'Swagger off in full view, you lucky Ordinaries! See if I care! I'm going back upstairs to my room to sleep some more, so that I'll be fresh for my afternoon with Mo.'

91

Directly above where the three conspirators had been talking, Cutie was lying on the floor of her room with her ear to a drinking-water glass. She had peeled the carpet off the floor, so that the glass, placed upside down with its rim flat against the wooden boards, amplified sound waves from the room below, enabling her to listen in to the conversation. So! she thought to herself. Annoying, am I? Well, I'll show you a thing or two, Dr Fancy-Pants Arvee! Your house-mouse girlfriend might be illiterate, but she knows enough not to dismiss me. And that makes her a whole lot smarter than you . . .

She remained in her room until Mo returned from her dance class and called out to her two pets. Cutie appeared wearing her most sober outfit, a plain grey pinafore and her hair – her real hair this time – arranged in a neat plait down her back. She behaved in a subdued, dignified manner. If Mo noticed the difference, she didn't mention it. The two mice stayed with the little girl until it was her bedtime. Then they wished her goodnight and went back to *Mercara*. Once behind the front door, Cutie went into the kitchen, made herself a cup of instant soup and went up to her room without another word. She didn't react even when Whee waylaid her on the stairs in a futile attempt to get a friendly pat or two. She just gave the beetle a shove and continued on up without so much as a whimper.

Arvee looked thoughtfully in the direction of the other mouse's retreating back, but decided to let well enough alone. At ten o'clock he got his gear together and prepared to leave *Mercarca*.

Watching covertly from her window, Cutie saw how Arvee stood on the windowsill, waving a torch around. She wondered what he was up to, until she saw the hugely elongated shape of a giant praying mantis appear, landing on the windowsill with a noisy clatter of wings. Ah-ha, she thought to herself. So he summons the insect using his torch! Easy-peasy. I can do that too!

She didn't wait to watch how Arvee mounted the unruly mantis. Opening her wardrobe, she asked herself, 'What's the most appropriate costume for an adventure these days? Hmmm. Shorts for sure – extra mobility. A halter top, in case it gets hot. And of course my white patent-leather thigh-highs, because I know I look gorgeous in them. A light jacket over the halter top, just in case it turns chilly, and a scarf for my head. *Voilà!* All done! Now for equipment. . . lemme see: opera glasses in case I need to look sharp, all-purpose nail file, basic make-up, perfume and – ooh! almost forgot! – deodorant. . .'

When she was done, she slung her tote bag over her shoulder and stood in front of the full-length mirror in her room. Yep! she thought. One cool mouse-cake! Dr Arvee, you're going to be proud of me – whether you like it or not!

13

TREETOP TERROR

Saturday Night

The glow-worms on the landing branch of the neem tree were blinking their welcome. But Arvee's mantis, Hungry Hilda, was in a feisty mood. Initially she refused to land at all and when she finally did set him down, it was on to the wrong branch.

'All right, Mr Mouse,' said Hungry Hilda, when Arvee got down. 'Fee-talk! Double the way, double the pay!'

'Excuse me?' said Arvee. 'That was *your* detour, not mine, and it cost you less than two minutes' delay!'

'Yah, yah! Delay-fillay!' said the insect in her harsh, grating voice. She had reared up to her full height, a good five centimetres taller than her passenger. 'Pay up and shut up – that's the mantis motto! Change of route, change of fee. Not my fault. Not my loss!'

She tossed her long, saw-tooth-edged forearms up in the air and cackled out loud. She looked tall and frightening in the shadows of the tree's leafy canopy. Dapples of moonlight filtering in through the leaves glittered in her bulging eyes. 'Double the air, double the fare! Hya-ya-ha-ha-ha!'

'Err . . . umm,' said Arvee. 'I'm really not very good at bargaining, you know, and all I've got is the one-way fare –'

'Arvee!' called a very welcome voice in the distance. It was Toon. 'Is she giving you grief about a fare increase?'

But Hilda was standing between the two mice. She threw back her small triangular head, then brought it down again swiftly. One set of tiny, razor-sharp teeth grinned out at Arvee now, suddenly at eye-level. 'Never been so close to a Mantis Airline's cash register, have you, little mouse, eh?' snickered Hungry Hilda, snapping her jaws together and twisting her head this way and that, as if sizing up her chances of a quick snack.

'N-now, let's just be reasonable,' said Arvee, standing his ground but wanting very much to back away.

'Reasonable, nothing!' stormed Toon from behind the insect. 'Come on – shoo! Scat, you oversized gnat! Either take what we're willing to give you or nothing!'

95

But Ellie had come up also. Shouldering her quick-tempered cousin aside, she spoke in what she hoped was a calming voice. Hungry Hilda had swung around and was now rearing up and down in an alarming manner above both mice. 'OK, compromise! Here's two-thirds the round-trip fare for your trouble,' she said, holding up two long strips of old ham. She flung them into the air towards Hilda. The insect, unable to resist the scent of food, immediately reared up and caught the snack in her forearms. 'We'll pay the final third on our way back to the house!'

The mantis, whose concentration was fuelled entirely by her hunger, screamed, 'Yah-yah! Sure thing! Yee-hoo-GLOMP! Yah-haaa-GLUMP!' She used her jaws to snap up the strips of ham and took off with them streaming out on either side of her head.

'Phew!' said Arvee. 'For a moment there, I thought I was larva fodder for sure.'

Ellie smiled. 'I always carry a little extra mantis money with me for those just-in-case situations! They've been making a lot of fuss recently.'

'Why are they suddenly asking for more?' asked Arvee.

Ellie said, 'Mine said she didn't want to land because she doesn't like this tree. Bad for insects, according to her.'

'Really?' said Arvee. 'Why would a tree be bad for insects?'

'Oh,' said Ellie, 'the smell perhaps. Humans use neem products for medicinal purposes. Twigs as toothbrushes, leaves as insect repellent, that kind of thing. I thought it only affected small insects, like sap-eaters and wood-borers. Not mantises.'

Toon shrugged. 'It's just hunger. Mantises need to eat. So they squeeze us for whatever they can get.'

'But why be nasty about it?' countered Ellie.

'Toon's got a point,' ventured Arvee. 'They don't think they're being nasty. They're letting their tummies do the talking.'

'Well, that's what I find depressing, then,' said Ellie, wrinkling her nose. 'The idea that, for some creatures, being horrid to other creatures is necessary for survival –'

'Well, it's not *all* creatures,' said Arvee, 'and I think we should be grateful for that.'

Suddenly, from below, there came a buzzing sound. Hum floated up, her antenna wiggling strenuously. She seemed very excited and a moment later had zoomed back down.

'Ooh!' said Ellie. 'That's the signal! They must have sighted the snake.'

The three mice scrambled down as fast as they could. All the other mice had already come out of the Web Room. They were lying flat on their tummies along the landing branch. Several lengths of looped rubber-band

97

bungee cords had been positioned strategically, for emergency evacuation if it became necessary. Bubble, Squeak and Lucky were sitting up on sentry duty, with slingshots, in case of owls. Toon, Ellie and Arvee quickly got into place, near Zero and Horse, who were closest to the tree's main trunk.

'It's moving slowly,' whispered Zero to Arvee, 'to avoid attracting attention, perhaps. Crax saw it about five minutes ago, coming from the direction of the Lantana Enclave. Then it circled around to the other side of the tree, where we can't see it from here. But if it wants to climb, it'll most likely come up this way, because the trunk slopes at a more comfortable angle from here.'

'Where is it now?'

'It's very difficult to see, because the central portion of the tree is under the shadow of its own leaves and the snake's black. But if you listen carefully, you can hear the sound of its scales. And, of course, there's that awful smell!'

From where Arvee lay, he had an excellent view of the front of the tree's trunk, though it was shrouded in darkness. But by tuning his ears carefully, turning them this way, then that, he began, uncertainly at first and then with increasing confidence, to focus upon the faint *slip-clicka-slip* rustling of the reptile's smooth, dry scales. 'I think it's started to climb!' whispered Arvee.

'Yes,' said Zero. 'I think so too. Just as I expected: up the front of the tree.' There was tension in her voice.

It was hard to be calm with a hungry cobra climbing towards you!

'And what about the snake repellent?' asked Arvee. 'Did you use my advice?'

'Well,' said Zero, 'Toon and Ellie described your plan, and we followed it as closely as we could. We used all the bits and scraps of smooth plastic we had. Only the colourless stuff, because we didn't want the humans to notice what we were up to, of course! But the construction workers had left a lot lying around. So it was easy. We stuck it to the tree's trunk using the sticky white glue that comes out of the euphorbia plants. The plastic covering extends about –' she made a quick calculation '– ten mouse lengths down from the entrance.'

'Good work!' whispered Arvee. 'That's close to a metre. Fantastic!'

'Arvee . . . you're quite sure snakes can't climb on plastic?' asked Zero.

Arvee sucked in his breath worriedly. 'Well, Zero,' he said, 'I've read that they can't climb on slick surfaces. Their scales need some irregularities in order for them to move forward, especially when they're climbing. Let's hope it's true!'

All the mice on the branch must have been holding their breath and listening with their ears strained to the utmost. In the silence, *clicka-clicka-rasp-rasp!* went the snake's scales against the tree's rough bark. *Clicka-clicka-rasp-rasp!* It moved with a rippling motion, one section of scales catching on the irregularities it found in the bark and pulling it forward, while the section behind bunched up. It was long, and so several sections moved simultaneously. *Clicka-click a-rasp-rasp! Clicka-clicka-rasp-rasp!* As it advanced up the tree, the terrible stench that preceded it became more pronounced. *Clicka-clicka-rasp-rasp!* And then, suddenly – *clicka-clicka-SNICK!* The welcome sound of scales losing their purchase on the slippery plastic.

'There!' breathed Arvee to Zero. 'Did you hear that?'

It was unmistakable. The young snake, close to two metres long, was coiled right round the tree's trunk, just beneath the covering of smooth, textureless plastic placed there by the mice. *SNICK!* went the sound of its scales as it tried to position itself on the plastic. *SNICK! SNICK! SNICK!* It was no use. It could go no further.

All the mice could hear the sound of the snake's difficulties by now. One by one, they were starting to stir. Arvee, still lying on his tummy, was staring hard at the section of the trunk where he thought he could see the snake's body coiled round the tree. He saw the head rearing away from the trunk. *SNICK!* went the head one last time.

And then . . . Arvee held his breath. The snake was starting to turn its head around. He could see it almost clearly now. It was starting to hiss. Uh-oh, he thought. It's mad at us. It's furious. And it can sense we're here. Arvee knew that snakes have the ability to sense movement at a distance, even when visibility is low. He wanted to yell to the other mice that they should stay down, not stand up. But his voice stuck in his throat. In the presence of a mortal enemy, one that even his Lab breeding could not cure him of, he was paralysed by fear.

Dimly, he could see the snake's head and neck begin to swell as its hood flared up. There seemed to be no deformity now. It was starting to sway from side to side. It was looking straight at the landing branch. It was hissing louder now and the terrible smell was very strong. Oh, no, thought Arvee. The idea of the snake being able to launch itself at the mice from the trunk of the tree was something he simply hadn't anticipated. If so, it was a serious miscalculation on his part. Ohnonononono, he thought, it's going to – *LUNGE!*

A dozen mouse voices squeaked aloud in terror!

And then the big black snake went whizzing harmlessly down, missing its target by a good metre. There was a loud thump as it hit the tree's trunk. Then a low moan and hissing groan.

Almost simultaneously another voice could be heard. Or was it just the snake talking to itself? It was hard to tell. The next sound was a very welcome one, of its scales again, but receding this time. Receding . . . receding . . . receding . . .

Gone.

14

THE SLINKING STINK

Saturday Night

Back at *Mercara* Cutie had discovered that it was no simple task to climb up a rope ladder wearing stiletto-heeled boots. By the time she'd reached the windowsill her hair was in complete disarray and her carefully lacquered whiskers were bent at awkward angles.

She fixed her face, then got out her torch to transmit a Mantis Flight calling code. 'How difficult can this be?' she asked herself. 'If those flea-wits can do it, so can I!' *Blinkety-blink!* she signalled, *blinkety-blankety-blink-blink-blink!* Within moments, she began to get results, but not the kind she wanted! The first arrival was a huge, bumbling, over-friendly moth who thought she was an exotic new flower. She'd barely succeeded in driving it away by spraying deodorant on to its antenna when a squadron of hunting mosquitoes, always on the lookout for a bit of fun, began dive-bombing her . . .

It was Whee who helped her out, finally. The beetle flew in from the neem tree, expecting to wait in *Mercara* for Arvee to come back. At the window ledge, instead of dipping under the mosquito mesh immediately, she stopped to watch what that new and rather unfriendly mouse was doing. Realizing that Cutie wasn't getting the mantis code right, the insect came over and attempted to teach her the correct rhythm by tapping on the mouse's shoulder with her antenna.

Cutie had got over her fear of the beetle, though she still didn't feel any fondness for the creature. 'Stop pawing me, you big black coconut!' she cried. 'Can't you see I'm trying to do something serious and complicated here?'

But Whee persevered, patiently tapping on the wall, rapping on the glass and on the window ledge. Finally, in desperation, she grabbed the torch from Cutie with her foreleg and tapped on it with her antenna.

'Ohh!' snapped Cutie, getting the point at long last. '*Why* didn't you say so from the start?'

Whee plunked the torch down with a long-suffering expression in her compound eyes and retreated a short distance away.

Blink-blink-a-blink-blink! signalled Cutie, *blink-blink-a-blink-blink! Blink-blink-a-blink-blink!* A few minutes later, the huge, looming shape of a mantis whirred in the air above her.

'About time,' said Cutie irritably. Slinging her tote bag over her shoulder, she prepared to mount the insect.

'Hey-hey-hey!' screamed the creature, whose name was Katy Ditzy. 'No pay, no way!' She was young and restless, with wings that flapped and clattered as if they had a life of their own. 'Where ya goin', Minnie Mousie? Around this garden we fix the fares before we airs!' She rather fancied herself as a poet.

'Oh, shut up,' snarled Cutie. 'Can't you keep your big, fat abdomen still? How's a mouse supposed to climb on with all this shifting and racketing about?'

It took all of Whee's antenna-waving diplomacy and promises of vast sums in deferred payment to stop the big mantis from zooming off into the night without Cutie. Even so, there was no way for Whee to advise the mouse about the need for rubber-band straps or any of the other precautions necessary to make a flight comfortable or indeed safe. Only with the greatest difficulty did the mouse finally get herself astride Katy Ditzy. And then, having nothing to hold on to, she fell forward, prone. With both her arms, she encircled the creature's abdomen and squeezed it tight.

Katy Ditzy sprang into the air with a wild cry, as Cutie's sharp, manicured claws poked into her soft undercarriage and the high-heeled boots dug into her sides. 'Yeeeeeeeee-owwwwwie! Owie! Owie!' shrieked the insect. 'Play rough, hang tough, Mousie Housie Pudding and Pie-eeeeeee!' She climbed steeply up towards the moon, then swerved, twiddling her wings this way and that, then banked to one side, then banked to the other side, tilted up, tilted down. Then she plummeted earthwards with her wings folded, which meant that Cutie was practically suffocated under the hard, tight wing cases.

Cutie screamed loudly, but it was futile. There was no one to hear her. Nothing in her life back at the Lab had ever prepared her for this experience. She'd seen the other mice boarding Mantis Arline flights and she'd assumed there was a fixed route and destination. This was, of course, far from true. The mantises were strictly mercenary. They had no training or education. They accepted passengers entirely upon their expectation of a fee. Katy Ditzy had flown the neem-tree route once or twice. So she flew in the same general direction, hoping that her passenger wanted to go there.

But when all she heard was one unbroken shriek, she lost focus entirely. Careening about the garden, heedless of where she went and how she got there, increasingly maddened by the pressure of Cutie's pinch-hold on her abdomen, she began to zigzag crazily, losing height, losing energy and ultimately losing interest. Finally she crash-landed on to the sturdy branch of a thorny euphorbia bush, hoping that the impact would knock her passenger off her perch.

It did. Very fortunately, instead of being skewered on the wicked thorns of the euphorbia, Cutie flopped sideways and down, landing on her back in the weeds growing all around the square-based flowerpot in which the bush had been planted. Terrified, bruised and hoarse with crying, the little white mouse crawled deeper into the cool, soothing thicket of stalks. But it was damp and dark. She stumbled into a sleepy centipede, which immediately curled itself up in a tight ball. A family of crickets, startled by Cutie's intrusion, sprang into her face with outraged chirrups.

In desperation, Cutie turned towards the garden. But the tall stalks of the grass and the bright moonlight shining down from above confused and dazzled her. Careless of where she went, she turned again and this time, she crouched low and plunged into the darkness. She hoped to find a quiet dry spot away from the grass, away from the pots, away from the open garden, where she could lie down and cry herself to sleep. In the morning, she told herself, when she could see properly, she'd find her way back to Mo and to *Mercara*.

Before she knew it, however, she'd run into a wall of some sort. It was the boundary wall. But Cutie didn't know enough about Paradise Villa to realize that this meant that she was as far from her home base as she could possibly get. All she knew was that there were weeds here too, and dampness and mould, and she couldn't go any further forward. It was very, very dark.

She was exhausted. Behind her was the garden, the hard bluish moonlight and the sharp-edged blades of grass. In front of her were darkness and slime. What should she do? She had no clue whatsoever!

She turned around. With the wall behind her, and careless of the effect it would have on her nice tote bag, she slumped slowly down till her tail was on the damp earth. I'm just going to sit here, she thought to herself, until I have a better idea.

She locked her arms round her knees and shut her eyes tight. For a very long time, nothing more happened. Cutie remained absolutely still. She didn't fall asleep. She could hear the sounds of the garden: of insects; of bats far overhead; of cars on the street beyond the boundary wall. She didn't know how long she'd have to remain like this, or whether she'd collapse from hunger and thirst before the morning dawned.

It was while she was seated thus, surrendered to her own misery, that she became aware of something approaching. It seemed enormously big, and it moved by sliding itself forward with a subtle, smooth-sounding rustling.

It was preceded by a smell. A smell like none she had ever encountered before.

Cutie's heart began to pound like a kettledrum. Her fur was standing up on end. She would have liked to cry, but no sound came from her throat. She would have liked to run, but every muscle in her body had turned to stone.

The sound and accompanying smell drew ever nearer in the terrible darkness.

Then the ghastly presence was directly in front of her.

A fog of white, sparking panic entered Cutie's brain, blanking out all thoughts. Then the creature stopped. Her eyes were still shut, but she could sense it looking at her. She imagined it had eyes of stabbing flame that flickered towards her. Any moment now it would touch her, pierce her, swallow her whole . . . The sensations she imagined were so real, she began to wonder whether she had already died. She had certainly stopped breathing.

It was in this state, through the pearly fog in her brain, that she heard a voice. It was a breathy, whispering voice clearly belonging to the animal in front of her. Strangely enough, hearing the voice had a calming effect on Cutie. It was soft and genteel, for one thing. And Cutie understood it, for another thing. She'd got top marks in Advanced Reptile-speak in school. The creature in front of her, she realized, was speaking a highly clarified but still recognizable version of that speech. With a slight lisp.

'Exthcuthe me, Mathter,' said the snake. 'There ith thomething here that may be of interetht to uth.'

'Really?' replied another voice, also speaking in Snake. But it was a hoarse, gruff voice, and it had a pronounced mammalian accent. 'Strange. I do not get even a whiff of its presence. Must be your overwhelming aroma, Stinky-Poo, my dear! Snuffs out all else in its path. Well, come on, then, describe the creature to me! As you know, my poor eyes are too weak to see anything in this light.'

'Ye*th*, Ma*th*er,' said Stinky-Poo. 'Ex*th*cu*th*e me if I he*th*itate. Thi*th* creature i*th* a mou*th*e, I think. But it look*th* a little different. It i*th* rather pale to begin with. Too pale for a mou*th*e. White, almo*th*t –'

'Just a moment,' said the mammalian voice. 'Did you say, white?'

'Ye*th*,' said the snake. '*Th*o far a*th* I can tell.'

'And . . . is it alive?' asked the one whom the snake called 'Master'. Even through the veil of her fear, Cutie could hear the excitement in the mammal's voice.

The snake sent a flickering probe in her direction. 'Ye*th*,' it said. 'Very definitely. I can *th*en*th*e it*th* heart. Beating very fa*th*t. But it'*th* not moving at all. I think it mu*th*t be a little bit *th*cared. I hope Ma*th*ter doe*th*n't mind me a*th*king . . . I*th* it *th*afe for me to eat a white mou*th*e?'

'Not just yet,' said the mammal, with what Cutie felt sure was a nasty smile. She wished she could raise her head to look at him. He didn't sound like a mouse and at the same time, whatever he was, he was definitely similar to a mouse. He seemed to be very close to the snake, perhaps even sitting astride it. 'Not just yet. I'd rather we spent a little time with him. Show him a little hospitality. Reacquaint ourselves with him. Oh, yes! I'm looking forward to this indeed! So if you don't mind doing the honours, Stinky-Poo, pick the mou*the* . . . uh . . . mouse up in your jaws and bring him along. And watch your fangs, please! I don't want him to suffer any harm. Not just yet anyway . . .'

'All right, Ma*th*ter,' said the snake in what seemed a resigned tone. 'A*th* you wi*th*h . . .'

Cutie fainted then. She'd heard all that she could bear to understand.

15

MOUSECUTiONERS!

Saturday Night

The first half-hour of the meeting was taken up with a heady, raucous celebration of the turning back of the fearsome serpent. Every mouse had a different version of where he or she was standing, and what thoughts had gone through his or her mind, and how wonderful that moment was when the terrible oppressor had finally fallen away.

'I don't think I breathed at all for five whole minutes!' cried Crax.

'Me neither,' echoed Feather, 'except I think it was ten!'

'And did you see the hood? I did!' said Heavy. 'It was *this* big! *Wah!*'

'And when he fell . . .'

'And when he went away . . .'

On and on ran the testimonials. Zero broke out a celebratory packet of peanuts she kept in store for special occasions. Each mouse munched on a whole peanut while Bubble and Squeak passed around a thimble of Daisy Honey wine, making sure that everyone got as much as they wanted of the sweet and mildly fizzy drink.

Finally, it was time to start the meeting.

'Two young mice belonging to the Granary family were taken yesterday,' reported Shane. 'Total number lost so far: nineteen.'

Zero explained to Arvee, 'We've been starting our meetings with a tally of missing mice. Today's report brings us up to date.'

'Over what period of time have the attacks taken place?' Arvee wanted to know.

'Since the end of February,' said Zero. She had a bit of paper on which she'd kept a record. 'Twelve weeks. I didn't start taking notes until after we moved here, but I *do* remember that we relocated one week after the first attack.'

'Three months,' said Arvee, looking troubled, 'that's a long time.'

'Many mice are growing desperate,' said Bizzy. 'Thinking of migrating. I must say I don't blame them.'

He had parents and three young brothers in Lantana Enclave. 'If they go, I suppose I'll go away too.'

'It's wonderful what we achieved today,' said Zero, turning to Ellie, Toon and Arvee. 'But how are we going to repeat this success on a large scale?'

'We're working on a three-step procedure,' said Ellie, 'of which we've completed the first one: safeguarding the neem tree.' Quickly, she outlined the other two. The mice listened attentively. When she was done, several paws went up in the air.

Shane spoke first. 'Ma'am, I'm not sure if I understood correctly – did you say we're tackling the shrews next? Shouldn't it be the snake?'

The other questioners nodded their heads, indicating that this was what they wanted to know too.

'After all, the snake's what's causing us the trouble. We need to go after it first.'

'Uh . . . well . . .' Ellie said. 'As we see it, the restrictions and regulations at Lantana Enclave are at least half as bad as the snake. If not for the restrictions, for instance, many of us could simply flee the colony until it was safe to move back there. But with the shrews hemming us in from all sides, we can't seem to take any decisions on our own. We're constantly at their mercy.'

There was a murmuring silence in the Web Room. It was Heavy who took it upon himself to express the thoughts of many mice when he stood up and said, 'Well, you know, Ellie . . . I can see that no one wants to be the one to say what's got to be said. What you've told us is fine and all. Yet, here's a creature that's actually, you know, tearing up homes and swallowing down innocents. That's just plain wrong. Shouldn't we do something more . . . direct about it? I mean, you know – can't we chase the snake down to wherever it lives, and . . . you know . . .' He shrugged, making a chopping motion with his hand.

'Oh, right,' said Zero. Her tone was heavy with sarcasm. 'Well done, Heavy. So now you want us mice to go around executing snakes! That's really ambitious! Ever thought about what's involved?'

Crax stood up. 'No one had heard of mice rising up against rats, organizing a rebellion and blowing up water pipes either – until we did it,' he said. 'That's what experience has taught us. That we can change the rules of reality, if we really want to.'

'Yes – but,' began Ellie. She kept looking towards Arvee, wishing he'd speak up. But he was looking down at his toes, tugging at his whiskers. 'Every creature has the right to its own life. Even creatures that harm us. Traditionally, we mice have followed the policy of avoiding or evading danger. Not *destroying* it –'

She was drowned out by a chorus of young voices calling out, 'But we did it with the rats!' and 'What's different now?' and 'Why must we be meek?'

Zero called for silence. 'Friends, as your leader I must admit to seeing both sides of the argument,' she said. 'But no clear decision is possible. My instincts are with Ellie.'

Toon spoke up now. 'I know Arvee doesn't agree, and I know now that Ellie doesn't either. But I believe we've got no choice but to get rid of the snake.' He turned towards Arvee. 'Doc, you're the one who first showed us that if we think logically and clearly, we can find solutions to our problems, even the worst of them. It was hard for some of us to change our ways, but now that we *have* changed, we can't return to being submissive!'

Arvee smoothed back his whiskers as he stood up. 'What you say is true,' he sighed, speaking to all the gathered mice. 'Don't misunderstand me, I don't have regrets. At the same time . . .' He look around. 'Friends, I believe we're in a unique position. If I had remained in my Lab, I'd still be writing papers on fruit-fly evolution, and raking my Zen garden. And you . . . well, you may all have continued living alongside the rats. As things happened, however, we met. As a result of that meeting, we've all been changed. I've been shown a great deal more about the real world outside my Lab and you've been shown what's possible when you stop being passive.'

He paused. 'Nevertheless, the solution we found to the problem of the rats wasn't a good one. It wasn't good because we used the methods of our enemies to defeat our enemies: we met violence with violence. And if we're going to become like them, then how can we call them enemies in the first place? I've been thinking a lot about that question. About activism and pacifism. But all I can say at this moment is that I have no suggestions to offer. If you're impatient to move ahead, I can't and won't stop you. At the same time, I won't pretend that I approve of your methods!'

He sat down again, looking sideways at Ellie. He hoped she understood that it was important for him to have taken this stand. She twiddled her whiskers at him in reassurance but said nothing.

Zero nodded as she said in her matter-of-fact way, 'Point well taken, Arvee! I'll note your reservations about whatever we do in the time ahead. However, the one point that stands out clearest from tonight's discussion is that we *must* regain access to Lantana Enclave. Whether we do that second or third isn't relevant.

'The key to the shrews' control over us is their method of keeping records. Using the ants. So here's what I propose: first we release the recorder ants. Frankly, I've been so disgusted at the way those poor creatures are suffering for the so-called security of Lantana Enclave's mice that I'd be glad to set them free as an end in itself. When we've got that done, we'll address the issue of the snake. Are we agreed so far?'

'Yes!' said all the gathered mice enthusiastically.

'Done,' said Zero. 'Thank you for your time, everyone. Feather? Ellie? Operation Ant Rescue is about to begin!'

16

THE PRETTY PRISONER

Saturday Night

Cutie awoke in a cool, dry place. She was lying down on a somewhat bumpy mattress made from a wad of bubble plastic stuffed into an old woollen sock. The mattress was on the floor of an underground room. There were no windows and its walls were of mud, lined with a double layer of bubble plastic to cut the damp. She moved her ears this way and that, trying to catch whatever sounds she could. She sniffed the air, wondering where she was. A trace of the horrid smell still lingered, but she appeared to be alone in the room.

She sat up.

Two fireflies captive in a small wire cage on the ceiling of the room blinked on and off alternately, providing a dim, flickering light. Beside the mattress was a side table made from a shiny brass medallion cemented on to the end of an empty film-spool. It was the only opulent touch in the otherwise bare surroundings. The door was made from an old audio cassette, cut open and the tape removed from it. The clear plastic viewing window now functioned as a vertical slit through which, when Cutie went up to look, could be seen a rough passageway. When she tried to open the door, however, she found it was locked.

Her tote bag had been placed upon the side table. She was still wearing her own clothes, including her boots, but someone had placed a robe made out of white brocade around her as an overgarment. It seemed considerably fancier than anything else in the room. It was soft and silky, with gold threads woven through it. At the neck, and at the wrists, tiny chips of mother-of-pearl had been sewn into place, shimmering prettily in the dim light.

Looking down at herself, Cutie decided she liked what she saw. 'If only I could get a full-length view!' she murmured. She dug into her tote bag to pull out the small, round hand mirror she always carried with her. But when she held it up to her face, she was dismayed to see that her fur was splotched with dirt. Her wig had fallen off and her real hair was in sore need of a shampoo. As for her whiskers, the straightening agent she used on them was wearing out, so that they were starting to frizz in the most ridiculous way! She got out a moist tissue and used it to scrub some of the dirt out of her fur. She surveyed the results in her hand mirror. Better than nothing, she thought.

A spasm of hunger wrung her stomach. Her throat felt parched. It was now almost four hours since she'd had her dinner snack in *Mercara*. She looked around the room, frowning. There was certainly nothing to eat in sight. Going to the door again, she used her nails to tap on the vertical viewing window. 'Hoi!' she called. 'Anyone there? I'm hungry! Thirsty! And I wouldn't mind a facial!'

It was too dark outside in the passage to see anything. However, she fancied that her words were greeted with an immediate scurrying, as of a cricket or an earwig leaving to summon a higher authority.

Sure enough, a few moments later she heard a restraining wire being unwound from the other side of the cassette-door. However, when it opened, there was no higher authority there. Only a young house mouse. His ears and nose were pointing down, his gaze averted.

'Oh, hello,' said Cutie breezily. 'Are you my attendant?' When he didn't answer, she sighed. 'No point expecting conversation from a house mouse, I suppose! Well, all right, then, fetch me some food and water – and a washbasin too! I'm absolutely filthy.' The other mouse continued to stand where he was.

'What's the matter, dummy?' said Cutie, starting to feel irritated. She grabbed the mouse's shoulders and gave him a shake. 'Come on! I saw your ears twitch. I know you can hear me.'

'He can *hear* all right,' said a deep, seductive voice.

Cutie jumped back instinctively.

'But he can't *answer*,' continued the voice. 'Such a shame. Born without a tongue, you know . . .'

By the light of the firefly lamp, Cutie could just make out a vast, bulky figure standing in the passage. From his voice, she recognized him to be the creature who had been riding the snake in the undergrowth. She guessed now, looking at his shape and height, that he was a rat. But he was unlike any she had known before.

The slender, silver-furred scholars who had occupied the Lab with her were practically a different species from the rodent who stood before her now. This one was huge and dark, exuding a raw, magnetic power. He was nearly twice as tall as Cutie, with a great bulbous nose and luxuriant black whiskers that reached almost to the floor. His voice was hoarse, as if he had a perpetual cold. But there was still something thrilling and hypnotic about it. The kind of voice that, once heard, is hard to forget.

'Allow me to introduce myself,' he was saying to her. 'My name is Pasha. I hope you've not found your accommodation too disagreeable? No doubt you're used to far, far superior circumstances!'

'The side table is smart,' said Cutie. 'Ethnic chic.'

Pasha sighed deeply. 'Ah! If only you could have seen my previous abode!'

'You moved recently?'

'"Moved"? Ah, no, my dear! Viciously evicted, is closer to the truth. By an act of monstrous villainy. A ruthless, murderous attack on my property, my people, my life . . .'

'Bummer!' said Cutie, wishing he would just get on with it and offer her some food.

'Forced to scrape together an existence for myself amidst the dirt and roots of the ugly earth! Defenceless, wounded and ill! I lost my wealth, my friends and even my eyesight, due to the terrifying fire that broke out in my underground palace . . .' As his emotions built up, his voice grew ragged and phlegmy. He wheezed heavily between breaths, then hawked and spat before finding his voice again.

Yuck! thought Cutie. For all his fine talk about palaces, Pasha's a crude dude!

He stopped short. 'Ah – but here I am rambling on about the vanished past without so much as offering the basic civilities! Tell me –' he seemed inclined to reach out to stroke Cutie's ears, but controlled himself '– tell me, my distinguished friend . . . what is your name?'

Cutie reacted speedily to her cue. Affecting a weak, undernourished tone, she said, 'Ohh . . . please . . . Mr

Pasha, I'm so-o-o grateful to you for saving me from the *darkness*! And the *damp*! My name's Cutie Pie – and oohh! I . . . I think I'm going to faint!' She half-swooned.

Her play-acting had the desired effect. Within moments, Cutie was being escorted from her little cell and into Pasha's own living quarters. The route they took was unlit. As she stumbled along in the rat's wake, she could sense the presence of at least four other mice. There were two on either side of Pasha, and one behind him, supporting his tail. The fourth mouse was the attendant who had opened the cassette-door. He offered Cutie a support to lean on, but she shook him off since she didn't really need it. All the mice appeared to be mute.

The stench, which had grown steadily as the small company walked along, was overpowering when they finally entered a long, low space, the further end of it obscured in darkness. Its ceiling and walls were covered with bubble plastic and curved, so that it was a bit like entering a barrel placed on its side and half-filled with earth. Sturdy metal hoops, which once belonged on bicycle tyres, held the bubble plastic in place. Bracing the hoops apart were the slender spokes of the tyres. Two huge wire chandeliers filled with softly blinking fireflies lit the front of the chamber.

On to the plastic had been stuck all manner of glittering, metallic items. There were bottle caps and the polished foil strips of expired medicines; rings from disposable fizzy-drink cans and shiny brass tacks; screws and bolts arranged in floral patterns. The floor was tiled solid with small-denomination coins, the spaces between them filled with window putty. Macramé mats made from shimmery brown audio-cassette tape and beads covered much of the floor, except for a central track running right through the middle of the room, from its entrance to the rear. On the left was a dining table made out of a solid slab of styrofoam, covered over with aluminium foil and mounted on four cutlery bone-handles. On the right, along the foundation bricks of the boundary wall, were tall stacks of matchboxes made into drawers and shelves.

Under the second of the firefly chandeliers was Pasha's throne. It had been constructed from an ornate papier-mâché stationery stand. The vertical sections had been cut out and repositioned to form a broad seat with armrests on either side. Its original indigo-blue colour, decorated with graceful gold and orange arabesques, had been augmented with swirls of sequins and decorative mirrors. Its bolsters were made from the separated fingers of what had once been a pair of men's leather gloves, stuffed with the ubiquitous bubble plastic.

When Pasha settled himself, grunting and wheezing, on to this magnificent seat, Cutie had to admit that he looked almost regal. Under the light of his chandelier, she saw that he was draped in several layers of gaudy brocade. On his head he wore a turban made out of a broad strip of pink chiffon. On his chest was draped a necklace of glittering ring nuts, alternating copper and brass. His eyes, however, were scarred over with a whitish membrane. He blinked constantly, and turned to his mouse attendants for help in locating objects or finding his way around.

'So,' he said, beaming at Cutie as one of the mute mouse attendants helped her into an easy chair made from the case of a travelling alarm clock, 'What do you think of my humble abode?'

She fluttered her eyelids. 'I've never seen anything like it,' she said truthfully. 'I hope we're going to eat soon.'

17

RECORD-ROOM RAID

Saturday Midnight

Two shrews were standing beside the sign outside the storage-box offices of the Neighbourhood Security Office. The sign had a single glow-worm positioned above it, lighting it up between blinks. 'It's a waste,' said the shrew called Mortis. 'Why bother with a sign when everyone knows where the office is?'

'Officer Diss says,' responded his twin brother, Rigor, 'it's to maintain the prestige of the office. "Mice can't function without obvious signage," says he. But then he gave the contract for producing the thing to a mouse! I ask you!'

'Wasteful. Decorative. Expensive.'

'Mind you, it's not as if any of us could've made it. Beneath us, that sort of stuff.'

'Manual labour.'

'Undignified.'

'But on the other hand, we're not the ones who need it! We already know whatever there is to know.'

'In my opinion – of course, no one asks for my opinion – the mice are turning out to be more trouble than we can afford.'

'Hear, hear!'

'Any news, by the way, of the fugitive?'

'The Stringer girl?'

'The one who came in here with the Freak.'

'Well . . . no. Not unless you count rumours.'

'I don't, of course – but tell me anyway.'

'I heard she was chased. By . . . the Dark One.'

'Really!' Rigor wheezed a laugh. 'That's an end to her, then!'

'Wasn't, though.'

'What! She survived?'

'Well . . . it's a rumour.'

'But how could she get away? No one gets away. It's unheard of. Unnatural. It's the fate of mice to submit themselves to the Dark One. Or else he'll turn on us.'

'Be that as it may.'

'Pooh! What a shame. Would've been one less mouse to worry about. They're a right nuisance, that's what I say. 'Course, no one listens to what I say. Oh, bother! Will you look at that? Here come two mice now.'

The shrews tried to pretend they were blind and deaf until they could no longer ignore the two mice standing directly in front of them.

'Excuse me, sirs,' said the first mouse, who was Ellie. But she had covered her hair with a scarf and was wearing a loose, flowing garment as a disguise. 'I need to make a registration for my friend.'

'Don't be ridiculous,' said Mortis, never dreaming that he was talking to the 'fugitive'. 'We're not open till sunrise.'

'Yes, sir, of course, sir, but I thought –'

'Mice don't need to think. Go away.'

'It's my friend, sir. She needs immediate medical attention.'

Mortis bared his small, sharp teeth. 'Well, she shouldn't be out in the open, then! Take her away!'

'I can't, sir – please – she's about to give birth.'

On cue, the other mouse, Feather, who looked as if she had a golf ball beneath her robe, began to clutch her belly. 'Ohhh – ohhh,' she moaned. 'Help me, help me – I'm having quadruplets!'

Both Rigor and Mortis jumped back several paces. They shrieked in unison, 'TAKE HER AWAY! It's bad luck for male shrews to have any contact with female events!'

'She's going to have them any minute, sir!'

'Call Officer Diss! He'll know what to do!'

'No! Call his wife! She'll know better!'

'Good idea!' screamed Mortis, over his shoulder, as he set off, running, 'I'll go and fetch her!'

'No, no, let me! I'm four seconds younger than you!' yelled Rigor in response, scooting ahead of him. 'I have less experience handling mice!'

Within moments, both shrews had vanished. Feather and Ellie stuffed their paws in their mouths to suppress their giggles. Then they got to work.

Feather quickly removed the toolkit strapped round her middle. 'We've probably got less than five minutes to get inside,' Ellie told her. 'I don't think it'll be difficult, though, to open the door of the office. Those two weren't expecting to leave their posts. They'll not have locked it tight.'

Sure enough, the office door had been secured with a simple wire twisted round a nail. Feather unwound the wire and both mice entered the darkened registration room, passing through the first storage box and into the next. The door to the third box had a recorder ant's cage nailed to it.

'This must be the room where the ants are stored,' said Ellie. 'You ought to leave now, Feather.'

'Ellie,' said the other mouse, 'I've been thinking. I'm probably better equipped for this task than you. There are close to three or four hundred wire cages in there, and I've had more experience with using the wire-clippers than you. I'll be quicker at it. Why don't you go back?'

'But I've lived at Lantana longer than you – I'm more used to shrews!'

Feather shook her head. 'If those two we met were typical, it'll make no difference at all. You or me, they'll throw us into the lock-up, with no questions asked, once they realize we were playing the fool with them. There's no time to argue! Now – please! Go.'

Ellie wiggled her whiskers in discomfort. 'I see your point, though I don't like it!' The other mouse was determined, however, so she relented. 'I'll have to lock the door from the outside, so that the shrews won't assume anyone's been in here,' she said. 'Be sure to cut open an escape hatch for yourself the first thing you do when you get in there . . .'

Hurriedly bumping noses, the two mice bade one another good luck before parting company.

Feather entered the storage room. She flashed her torch around. The place was packed tight, floor to ceiling, with the tiny wire cages of recorder ants. All the cages had been covered with gauze, stacked in pairs, back to back, and the stacks arranged in rows. Though she could not see the ants, lying in suspended animation within their cages, Feather could smell them: dry and sour, with a trace of sadness. She could hear the faint rustling sound of countless little insect bodies expanding and contracting as they processed the stale air of the room.

By the door was a large rubber-stoppered glass jar and inside it was a hardened lump of honey. 'I better get started,' murmured Feather. 'I'll do ten ants at a time – cut open their cages, feed them the honey and place them on the floor. That way, they'll be able to escape the moment they get to their feet.'

She looked at the watch that Arvee had lent her. It was ten minutes to three, so she had two and a half hours before daybreak.

She knelt on the floor and, using a pin, punched out a pattern of holes in the hard plastic wall of the storage-box room. She made a rectangle large enough so that she could pass through it too. Then, using a fragment of box-cutter blade, she sliced the spaces between the holes, following the line of perforations. When three sides were done, it was a simple thing to push down the flap she'd created. The result was a mini-ramp of sorts, leading out from the floor of the Record Room into the soil and grass outside. So long as she kept her torch turned off, no one would notice the hole in the central box of the six that made up the Neighbourhood Security Office. She had to work in total darkness. But with her nose and whiskers to help her, she knew she'd manage.

She'd just snipped open the thin wire cages of the first ten ants, when she heard the sound of Rigor and Mortis returning. They were still some distance away. Apparently they'd managed to raise both Officer Diss and his wife from their sleep.

Feather opened the honey dispenser and dipped her left paw in. Using her claws, she scraped at the hardened lump of sweetness that half-filled the bottle. Then, feeling her way with care, she inserted her right paw into the first of the cages she'd opened and drew out the inert body of an ant. Lightly daubing its tiny mandibles with honey crystals, she set it down on the mini-ramp and moved on to the next cage. When she'd released ten ants, she got out her wire-cutters and opened another ten cages.

Outside, the shrews were drawing close. Feather could hear their voices.

'They threatened us,' Mortis was saying.

'With quadruplets,' said Rigor.

'There was nothing we could do,' said Mortis.

'Alone against the quadruplets,' said Rigor.

There was an incoherent snarl from Officer Diss.

Mrs Diss whined, 'But it's not our *job* to come out at night!'

Rigor said, 'A scandal! That's what they wanted to cause, bursting with quadruplets in the middle of the night!'

'No shame, these mice,' said Mortis.

They had reached the signpost. There was a slight pause.

'I see no mice,' said Officer Diss, in a dangerously mild voice. 'Shameless or otherwise.'

'I don't see anyone!' shrilled Mrs Diss.

Mortis was making gulping sounds, as he if were trying to swallow his own whiskers. 'Guhh, guhh . . . but they were *right here*, sir!'

Rigor said, 'Full of quadruplets, sir!'

There was another pause. 'If you mention those quadruplets once more, Rigor,' said Officer Diss, 'I'll quadruplet *you.*' There was a strangled, choking sound. The senior shrew had picked his two subordinates off the ground by the collars of their uniforms. 'Now get this straight, you two fiddle-headed prunes! If you ever – and I mean *EVER* – break down the door of my residence, in the middle of the night, squawking about an invasion of phantom pregnant mice again, I'll throw you into a wire cage with the ants! D'you hear me?'

'And never give you any honey!' squeaked Mrs Diss, in a voice so high she sounded like a bat.

'But – but – but,' spluttered Mortis.

'Not a word,' snarled Officer Diss. 'Not another word.' He turned and left, with his wife emitting ultrasonic complaints all the way.

Inside the Record Room, Feather worked slowly and methodically through the cages, smiling to herself as she listened to the shrews. The first of her ants had revived. She heard a skittering sound as its spindly feet struggled to find purchase on the smooth plastic surface of the ramp. Though she couldn't see the small creatures, she imagined them coming to their senses, standing up and staggering about for a few seconds.

She imagined them flexing their antennae, bending their countless joints and looking around with their compound eyes, before deciding that their best course lay in going towards the fragrance of the fresh air and moist earth outside. Once there, they would fan out in the grass until in due course one of them found a scent trail that belonged to their ancestral nest. The first one to find that trail would leave a new trail of scent behind it, which would in time be found and followed by another ant and then another and another, until all of them, eventually, would return to their own home nest.

She wondered whether they felt curiosity or dread or relief.

I suppose I'll never know, she thought to herself, as she started out on her fifth set of ten wire cages. It was very hard to believe that they felt anything at all. Ants had always seemed like tiny mechanical beings, with no clear-cut individuality or sense of their own personal fate. Nevertheless, as she set each diminutive body down on the ramp, and she heard the pattering sounds of each insect as it returned to consciousness, she had the strongest sense that each one, in its miniature way, understood the whole gladness of being alive.

18

HUNGER IN THE DARK

Saturday Post-midnight

Cutie and Pasha were waited upon by the mute mouse attendants as they ate their meal. Cutie was too hungry to mind that it was composed almost entirely of grilled earthworm and steamed daisy roots, though there was a bit of real coffee liqueur to wash it down with. Pasha did most of the talking, describing his days of glory and contrasting them with his current reduced status. He claimed to have been born in a famous Laboratory, from which he was turned out once he was no longer of use to science. Ever since then, he said, he had yearned to return to those days of 'elegance, learning and dignity'.

Finally, the food was cleared away.

'My dear Cutie,' said Pasha, 'I hope you will allow me the liberty of using your first name?' She fluttered her eyelids appealingly. 'It has been the most wonderful privilege, having you here as my guest. I am sure you have many provocative and delightful activities with which to fill your glamorous life, so I am loath to detain you any longer than is strictly necessary.'

Cutie fluttered her eyelashes again. What a relief, she thought. He's getting ready to say goodbye. I *do* hope he offers to drop me home . . .

'Nevertheless, there's a tiny favour I'd like to ask of you. Naturally, it has no connection with my rescuing you from certain death in the dangerous undergrowth! No connection at all. . .'

Cutie registered a blip of annoyance on the screen of her mind. Uh-oh, she thought. How boring. He's going to want something in exchange for saving me. Out loud, she said, 'Why, of course! Anything you say!'

Pasha stroked his whiskers. 'As I am sure you agree, this damp underground location is demeaning to a creature of my eminence. I have, for some time, been developing a scheme that may restore me to my rightful position! But I cannot achieve my goal without help. I was wondering . . . assuming it would not be too taxing . . . if you would be interested in lending me a fraction of your intelligence, your expertise and, of course, your exquisitely unusual appearance towards that end.'

The mouse twiddled her whiskers prettily. 'Oh! You're too kind! But I'm looking such a mess just now.'

'No pearl could do more grace to an oyster,' said Pasha, pretending he could see quite well, 'than your perfect whiteness in the squalor of my home!'

Cutie's nose went bright pink with pleasure. 'Thank you! Of course, I'm not sure what poor little me can do to help.'

'You would make the difference between grand success and dismal failure. What I need, specifically, is someone who would be willing to play the role of a . . . how shall I put it? A spiritual leader. A popular icon. A celebrity. Yes – I can tell from your reaction that the idea appeals! Your responsibility would be no more, no less, than to allow yourself to be worshipped by a whole garden of adoring devotees. You would be an inspiration to them. Poets would write songs in your praises and sculptors would carve your likeness into every snail's shell.'

'Ooo!' breathed Cutie. 'That sounds like super fun! I've always wanted to be a performer! Could I dance too? I can write my own songs and everything!'

Pasha nodded, smiling, but what he said was, 'Naturally, you'd have to follow my instructions about what to say. After all, I've been planning this . . . uh . . . spiritual revival, for a little while now.'

Cutie's brow clouded over. 'Aww! Couldn't we make it a double act? I could sing and dance, then you could follow on with your lecture.'

'Dearie me, no! I can't appear at all. Not for some time, anyway. Wouldn't want to frighten the little devotees, after all! You, on the other hand, would charm them and beguile them, while saying whatever I wished them to hear. I mean, of course,' he added hurriedly, 'you could have your own variety programme too, eventually.'

'Oo!' said Cutie, getting to her feet to do a little pirouette right there and then. 'I could train a troupe of crickets and maybe a cicada or two to play the accompaniment – and we could have rows and rows of glow-worms – and a box office! We *must* have a box office – and send out invitations – even to *Mercara*! It'll be *such fun*!' Her eyes were sparkling. 'I can't wait to see Arvee's face when I first appear . . .'

Pasha's tail twitched violently. 'Ah!' he said. 'You *do* know him, then? I wondered about that.'

'Why, of course,' said Cutie, matter-of-factly. 'He's my fiancé!'

Pasha's damaged eyes narrowed. 'How . . . interesting.' 'You know him too?'

'My first thought, when Stinky-Poo described you to me, was that you *were* the famous doctor. But no, sadly, I didn't know him well. We met on a few occasions. He enjoyed my hospitality for a couple of weeks. But he left without saying goodbye. Rather rude of him, I thought.'

'Hmm, yes, he can be a bit rude. But that's only because he's a scholar! Scholars are often quite rude, I've noticed. They can't seem to help themselves.'

'Indeed, yes, he is an exceptional animal. I should very much like to re-establish contact with him. I believe I have a couple of small scores to settle.'

'Well, you can send a personal invitation, then,' said Cutie, her mind already working on the details of the costume she would wear. 'I'm crazy about him! He's *so* handsome, don't you think? Except that he's been bewitched by that ugly little house-mouse girlfriend of his. Do you know her too? I've been desperate to break her hold over him – and this show will be just the perfect event!' She twinkled her whiskers. 'Don't you think?'

'Oh, yes,' said Pasha. 'Oh, absolutely.'

'Well, that's settled, then. When do we start? I'll have to rehearse a routine, you know. It'll take me a couple of days. Speaking of which –' she glanced around '– you wouldn't happen to have a clock anywhere, would you? I'll need to be getting back. To my home, I mean. To my human. She wakes up around six, you know, and I . . . uh . . .' She stammered to a halt. 'Wh-why? What's the matter? Did I say something wrong?'

Pasha's tail was lashing about uncontrollably. 'Not a thing, my dear,' he said, though he was breathing heavily. He coughed and cleared his throat noisily before continuing. 'I'd have thought, though, a clever mouse like you would realize I couldn't possibly let you go right now. Not until you'd performed my little task.'

Cutie stared at him. '*Not go?* Oh, but. . .' Her tail curled instinctively round her ankle. 'I *have* to, don't you see? My human friend, Mo, will miss me.'

'So will we,' said Pasha. 'But don't worry. It shan't take more than a few days. A week at the most –'

'A week!' cried Cutie. 'That won't do at all. She'll think I'm lost! She doesn't know that I left the house. She'll come looking for me.' She stopped. Then, in a more cunning voice she said, 'I'm sure you wouldn't like that? I mean, I don't know much about the world, but I think – I've been told – that humans can be quite unkind when it comes to, you know, what they call "pests".'

'Quite right!' said Pasha, nodding. 'They hate rats! They do their best to exterminate us! However . . .' A nasty grin was beginning to spread across his face. He reached up, pulling on a cord that hung from the ceiling and vanished towards the darkened space behind his throne. 'I believe there are certain creatures that humans not only detest but are also irrationally afraid of. No doubt you are aware of this fact?'

Cutie's fur began to stiffen automatically. The ghastly stench that had been present all along was suddenly stronger than ever before. There came the sound of smooth scales slipping across the coins on the floor.

'My guess,' said Pasha, his voice ever more throaty, 'my guess is that our young friend Stinky-Poo might be one of those creatures. Perhaps you will remember meeting him a short while ago? Just before you fainted, as I recall. You owe him a debt of gratitude, my dear. He is the one who transported you to my shelter. In his mouth. Of course, I exercise a tight control over him. When we first met, he permitted me to hypnotize him, so that he cannot swallow unless I give him the command.

'It's a small price to pay for the debt he owes me in the matter of saving his life. The poor wretch was starving when I found him. On account of his atrocious bad breath and the attendant lack of self-confidence it caused, he can never catch any prey. Naturally he tried to eat me, the poor brute. But I talked him out of it by suggesting a means by which we could help one another. If he would help me regain my control over . . . uh . . . *ordinary* mice, I would provide him with an unlimited supply of small victims. Alone, we are dysfunctional – me with my blindness, he with his bad breath. But together we make a formidable team!'

Cutie stepped back a pace. Her heart was beating fast again.

'The humans never seem to understand that poor Stinky-Poo, like most snakes, has no interest whatsoever in them! He can't eat them, after all. Nevertheless, I do believe that if your young human or her parents had the slightest notion that a cobra inhabited the undergrowth, they would be most unwilling to venture into it. Even to retrieve one so precious and beloved as you.'

The slippery, sliding sounds were no longer advancing. Instead, there came the deep in-drawn hissing of breath. Cutie looked up.

Rising above the ornamental backrest of Pasha's throne was the spreading hood of the young cobra. The pale, creamy scales of his throat glistened in the dim light, as his handsome dark head curved down over the top of the throne. His long purple tongue, forked and muscular, flickered out again and again, tasting the air, picking up traces of scents and chemicals that communicated a world of delicate precision to him.

'Did you call me, Ma*th*ter?' he hissed plaintively. 'I*th* it time to eat?'

19

'DANGERANiUM MOUSENARiES'

Sunday

Arvee took a Mantis Airline flight back to *Mercara* once Ellie and Feather had set off on their mission. He had a couple of hours to himself before Mo woke up. *Mercara* was mercifully silent as he crawled in through the piano-room window. He was glad, thinking it meant that Cutie was curled up safely in her bed and peacefully asleep. But as he passed her room on the way up to his own, he saw to his dismay that the door was open and she was nowhere in sight.

'Oh, no!' he murmured. 'What does this mean?'

She hadn't left a note to say that she planned to go out. There was no sign of a struggle or forced entry. The house appeared to be exactly as he remembered leaving it. Arvee stepped into Cutie's room. Her clothes were strewn all over. But they had been like that on the morning of the previous day too. In one corner, she had set up a dressing table. Next to it were three wig-stands. One had a hairpiece on it, coiffed and ready to wear. The second one looked as if it had been run over by a lawnmower. This, he realized with a pang of guilt, was the one he had whisked off her head by mistake the previous morning. The third wig-stand was bare.

He looked around the room. No sign of the wig. It would be typical of Cutie to dress up like a Christmas tree even when setting out on an adventure!

'This is *so* vexing!' he said to himself. There was no one available to help with a search. Back at the neem tree, only Sparx and Bizzy would be awake, keeping watch until Feather and Ellie returned. Everyone else had decided to turn in for the night. The only thing Arvee could do, perhaps, was to signal up a Mantis Airline flight. But it was getting close to dawn and the insects avoided flying in daylight.

Every bone in his small body felt tired. If I don't rest now, he thought, I'll be a dormouse all of tomorrow. He went up, brushed his teeth, crawled under his duvet fully clothed and fell asleep instantly.

An hour later, his alarm clock buzzed like an angry bee in his ear. For an instant, when he opened his eyes, he wondered where he was. He'd been dreaming about Ellie soaring above the clouds with her ears outspread like wings and pale blue wigs galloping around the garden. He sat bolt upright. Cutie! The galloping wigs reminded him of her. Had she come back?

He leaped out of bed and tore downstairs to the guest room. It was still empty.

'Oh, my whiskers,' he muttered to himself. 'This is going to develop into an all-out crisis.'

There was still a little space of time before Mo came to switch on the Japanese lantern over *Mercara*. Of course, it's not as if she'd need to see both of us right away, thought Arvee. Cutie was a late riser and usually did not surface immediately. It wouldn't be strange for him to spend a little friendly time alone with Mo in the morning. But after that?

As it was Sunday, the little girl would be home all day. There would be no escape. Arvee would have to stay in all day too. Whee was in the house, so he'd be able to send a message back to the neem tree with her, requesting the others to send out a search party for the missing white mouse. But he wouldn't be able to go himself. Instead, he had to solve the immediate problem of how to pass the hours while Mo was at home without making it obvious to her that one of her pets was missing.

Arvee was still standing in Cutie's room, thinking about his problem, when he saw himself reflected in the full-length mirror in the middle of the room. Behind him, he could see the dressing table and wig-stands. Cutie was the same height as him. The same weight. Suddenly he groaned aloud and clutched his ears: an idea had dawned on him, but he wished it hadn't! It was so ridiculous!

A short while later, however, Arvee found himself standing in front of Cutie's mirror, feeling quite amused. He was the perfect replica of the other mouse: he was wearing her wig, a tight black T-shirt and a long blue skirt which flowed down to his toes. He'd put on a pair of her ridiculously high heels and had coloured his nose an unnatural shade of bright pink. The only touches he'd not been able to add to his appearance were the false eyelashes. He'd struggled for at least ten minutes with them, but each time had ended up with what looked like black furry caterpillars stuck to the insides of his ears. So he left them off.

He had better success with Cutie's blue contact lenses, which she had left behind. They reminded him of the time when, in Ratland, he had worn tea-dipped lenses and coloured his fur brown, in order to pass for one of the house mice. When he'd popped Cutie's lenses into place, tilted his head to one side and blinked rapidly a few times, he looked so startlingly like Cutie that for a moment he wondered if it was her, and not him, reflected in the mirror.

Wearing his disguise, he spent the whole morning with Mo, then later switched back to himself in the afternoon. She didn't seem to notice the difference. He was grateful that, for all their advancement, humans had almost no ability to identify a creature by its smell. No animal, he knew, would be fooled for very long by his little trick. Though he was wearing Cutie's perfume and her clothes, his scent would eventually assert itself over hers.

At midday, Hum returned to *Mercara* with cheerful chirrups. She had a message tied to her back leg confirming that Feather had successfully released all the ants in the Record Room and returned to the neem tree. Developments were being awaited, Toon wrote. Meanwhile, Ellie wrote to say that one of the mice had made a disturbing discovery: an unfamiliar bluish object had been recovered from the garden and brought back to the neem tree. She had immediately recognized it as one of Cutie's wigs. It had been recovered from near the outer boundary of the Lantana Enclave, near the first of the euphorbia pots.

Arvee had already sent a message earlier, via Whee, explaining that Cutie was missing. Now he wrote to say she had still not returned and that he'd be grateful if efforts could be stepped up to find her. Then he sat back, feeling frustrated. He wished he could be the one looking for her, because she was his house guest and therefore his responsibility. She could be in serious danger, what with a cobra on the loose. But he couldn't leave *Mercara* until evening. All he could do was hope that she had enough survival instinct to get herself out of any really bad scrapes and that she would be found before Mo realized she was lost.

Back in Lantana Enclave, Officer Diss was holding a crisis session at the Neighbourhood Security Office.

His room was in the tallest and most spacious of the storage boxes, fitted with numerous bits of furniture confiscated from the mice. His desk was a slab of styrofoam built up on matchbox shelving. He sat in a swivel chair carved out of a tennis ball and mounted on ball-bearings. On the wall behind the desk were sections of film negative, framed in plastic slide-jackets. No images were visible, of course, but abstract designs had been scratched into the emulsion. Empty matchbooks had been turned into files for holding paw-print records. Paper clips had been threaded through each file, and all the files had been slung from a wire looped along both the side walls of the box. The flooring had been created out of old Scrabble tiles.

Six sub-inspectors squatted in a row on the floor, as there were no chairs for them. Their names were Murk, Dwindle, Callous, Furtive, Sneak and Turgid. They were variously chewing their whiskers, fidgeting with the tips of their tails and digging wax out of their ears.

Diss was sitting in his swivel chair, looking fierce. 'Six sub-inspectors,' he snarled, 'and not a single one of you could prevent over three hundred ants from being released!'

Murk spoke up at once. 'Sarr,' he began, speaking in a strong, countrified dialect. 'Dangeranium mousenaries were detectivated h'operating near this h'orifice on the very nightie of the h'attack –'

'Yes, yes,' muttered Diss, 'I know all about the mousenaries – one and a half pregnant females! Those witless sentries came running to wake me up at the time of the "attack" and left the orifice – uh – office unguarded! But the fact remains we were unable to prevent the vandals from destroying the records. Frankly, I don't give a beetle's click about the records, or anything else to do with these pesky mice. If I had my own way, we'd go straight back to our part of the garden – in the back, near the kitchen sewage. A much better residential area, in my opinion, being closer to the source of food, and less cluttered with plants and other natural rubbish.'

His smooth fur was suddenly wrinkled with concern. 'But we can't have our own way any more. We lost that option from the time we agreed to help the . . . the . . .' He stopped and mopped his brow. 'Our Supreme Commander.'

Furtive said, 'Sir, we cud allus pretend that nutting hoppinged. To the h'ants, we means.' He looked around at the others. 'We's not telling tales. Promise.'

Diss glanced in his subordinate's direction. He knew he couldn't trust any of them. If he didn't report the break-in to Pasha, his sub-inspectors would do it behind his back, and would be well rewarded for their pains. He should know, after all. That was how he had risen to his position. He said, 'Oh, yes, I'm sure you won't. Nevertheless, I can't run the risk that one of you might be caught and tortured till you squealed. No, there's no way round it. We've got to tell him. And he's going to be angry. I don't want to even imagine how angry.' He began to suck on his claws in distress. If only he could run away.

'Excuse me, sarr,' said Murk. 'H'I believe h'I have a solutionary.'

'Oh?' said Diss.

'We'll say that h'our bravid sentricurity force fought a ferocitous battle-arum for the h'orifice, resulting in the deathness of the mousenaries. In the course of the battle-arum, the recordible antics were lost . . .'

Diss had to concentrate hard to understand his subordinate's speech. 'No, no!' he said. 'That'll only mean he'll insist on seeing the bodies of the mice so that he can feed them to –' He stopped. 'Oh, wait. He won't do that. His horr – . . . uhh . . . glorious companion needs *live* prey. If we say that the wretched mousenaries were *killed* in an encounter, he won't need to see them!'

'My point h'exackly, sarr,' said Murk, looking smug.

20

A FATAL MISTAKE

Sunday

Cutie spent the remainder of Saturday without food or water. By Sunday morning it had become clear to her that she was meant for greater things than a slow death by starvation in the clutches of a nasty, bullying rat. She agreed to play along with Pasha's scheme.

'It makes me very glad, my dear,' said Pasha, 'to find that you've come to your senses. It would have been a shame to have to use my special methods of persuasion upon you.' He squinted at her with his weak eyes. 'Even with my sadly reduced vision, I can see that you're glowing like a movie star!'

She was wearing a shimmering white robe that glittered in the greenish, pulsating light of the fireflies. The mute mouse attendants had helped her to wash her white fur till it sparkled now with a light of its own. The robe was cut away so that her neck and arms and back were bare. Clearly, the colour of Cutie's fur was to play an important part in the performance that lay ahead.

The mouse attendants had brought a long mirror fashioned out of a strip of reflective film for her to admire herself in. She was very pleased with what she saw. Turning this way and that, she caused the gauzy material of the robe to float round her so that at times it seemed as if she had wings.

'Have you, I wonder,' murmured Pasha, 'memorized the details of what you'll say and do?'

'Of course,' said Cutie. 'I took notes. Will there be time for a rehearsal?'

'Heavens, no! Our friend Stinky-Poo would collapse from the tension.'

'Ohh!' pouted Cutie. 'That's so *unprofessional!*'

'It's not prudent to test a cobra's endurance beyond a certain limit.'

'How can you be sure there'll be an audience?'

'Nothing to worry about in that department!'

'Has Arvee been invited?'

'I'm sure he'll have heard about the . . . uh . . . show tonight. If he's smart, he'll be there.'

'What about afterwards? Will there be time for curtain calls?'

'Let's put it this way: there won't exactly be a curtain, but then again your adoring audience will have ample opportunity to come up to you and pay tribute. If you follow your instructions carefully, it'll all go smoothly and at the end of that time you'll return safely to our underground retreat.'

Cutie drew in a breath. 'And,' she began tentatively, 'how soon afterwards may I go home?'

'Let's not worry our pretty little head about such minor issues,' said Pasha. 'It'll happen in its own good time.'

Cutie shrugged, but in the privacy of her thoughts she added, Meany!

'I'll leave you now,' said Pasha. 'I have a couple of visitors awaiting me in my audience chamber. Be sure to get some rest now! It's going to be a long evening.'

He left her and swaggered into his audience chamber. His visitors had been standing all the while. They were Officer Diss and two sub-inspectors, Murk and Dwindle. All three grovelled and folded their ears down as Pasha passed them, with his mouse attendants on either side to keep him from stumbling. When he had settled himself on his throne, he said, 'OK, let's hear it.'

'Sire,' said Diss, 'the arrangements are in place.'

'Oh, of course they are, you witless cocoon! I meant, what news of the vandals who demolished your Record Room? Have they been caught? Have they been flogged?

I have a very hungry cobra in my back room – and there's nothing more he likes than a bit of live, well-flayed mouse-meat!'

Murk coughed. '*Eheu!* Well, sarr,' he began, 'the vandalarums were taken into custardy, but I regrotto to say –' he coughed several more times '– they . . . errr . . . they have h'expirated. *Eheu! Eheu!* ' He placed a paw over his pointy nose. 'Sarr will h'excuse pliss! My 'umble self suffers 'orribly – *eheu! eheu!* – from h'asthmum when venturizing h'underground. *Eheu! Eheu!* '

'Excuse me,' said Pasha in a dangerously polite tone. 'Did you say . . . did you mean to say . . . that the vandalarums, as you call them, have "expired"?'

'*Eheu!* Yessar. H'expirated. *Eheu! Eheu! Eheu!* Parcelled on to an 'igher planarium. Deadimus. *Eheu!* '

'I see,' said Pasha, nodding his huge head. The expression on his face was quite gentle.

Officer Diss had been trying, unsuccessfully, to suppress Murk's tendency to talk too much. But now he relaxed. The rat seemed to be in a benign mood after all.

Pasha reached up and pulled on the cord that hung down from the ceiling. 'I'm sorry to hear that,' he continued, in what seemed to be a friendly tone of voice. 'But then again, it isn't such a tremendous loss. After all, Stinky-Poo isn't very fussy.'

Diss's short, stubby whiskers began to vibrate with alarm. He realized he may have misjudged Pasha's mood after all. When he heard the sound that caused his nose-hairs to shrink, he was sure of it: *clicka-clicka-rasp-rasp* . . . The smooth, slithering sound of the cobra's scales as it emerged from its lair behind Pasha's throne.

Clicka-clicka-rasp-rasp . . . Clicka-clicka-rasp-rasp . . .

There was a pause while it gathered its energy to raise its body upright and spread its hood. And there it was in all its menacing glory, swaying above Pasha's head, its ghastly tongue flickering in and out. 'Ye*th*, Ma*th*ter? You called?'

'Indeed, my pet,' said Pasha, in an oily voice. 'You see before you three shrews. One of them, I'm afraid, suffers from a rather dreadful case of asthma. I believe you have a cure for his affliction. A very *final* cure. Let's see if you can identify which one of the three is the sufferer? Yes! Clever Stinky-Poo! It *is* the one who's trying to run away! Good boy! Well caught! Now, now – don't be impatient, I'm going to let you eat it this time. So, TAKE IT, there's a good snake, TAKE IT!'

Officer Diss and Sub-inspector Dwindle were prostrate on the floor, their teeth chattering in abject fear, their eyes shut tight. From far away, it seemed, the sound of muffled coughing and *'Eheu! Eheu! Eheu!'* could be heard for several moments. Finally it was stilled.

'Now, then,' said Pasha, in the same pleasant voice, 'let us forget this sorry incident and pass on to more attractive matters – tonight's programme, in short. Diss, I hope you have taken careful note of what happens to those who do not follow my orders closely.

What's that? Can't speak for chattering teeth? What a shame. Well, I'll just have to assume you've understood everything, then – and that the construction of the access tunnel is complete, that the performance space has been correctly prepared, that the moonlighting meets our exacting standards.

'Naturally, I will come on a tour of inspection shortly to satisfy myself that all is in order. For the moment, you may go. No need to stand if that's not possible just now. Crawl away on all fours if you want – it's quite an amusing spectacle! I may insist that you adopt that posture at all times henceforward!'

Ellie's map of the garden was spread inside the Web Room, held in place by eight obliging glow-worms. All of the Neem Tree Gang apart from Feather and Sparx sat or stood, looking towards Ellie, Toon, Arvee and Zero, who were gathered near the centre.

Ellie directed the beam of her torch at the map. 'As you can see,' she said, 'this is a map of the garden. No one has been able to go in or come out of the colony today on account of the curfew, but a few messenger ants have begun to operate again, since we released them from the Record Room. They've brought information about a public meeting that's been called this evening, at this spot.' The map showed the fifteen lantana bushes of the

Enclave. Between the sixth and the seventh Ellie had marked a space in red. 'It's roughly in the middle of the Enclave. Security will, of course, be very tight, but Toon and the others have been busy devising disguises. Yes?' Whizzbang and Spud had put up their hands to ask a question.

'What is supposed,' said Whizzbang – 'to be happening tonight?' continued Spud. The twins often spoke in this combined fashion.

Bizzy answered, 'Nobody knows for sure. The shrews have been deliberately mysterious. Frankly, I think most of them don't know themselves.'

'It's going to be a show, that much is certain,' said Toon. 'Last night, while Feather and Ellie were on their mission, Zero and I called up two Mantis Airline flights and buzzed over the Enclave. The area marked in red on Ellie's map has been cleared of grass and leaves. To the rear of the bare patch of earth, on the side closer to the boundary wall, there's a *something*, but we couldn't see much. It might be a hole. Or it might be a platform. It seemed to be covered with leaves. We'll only know for sure tonight.'

'If it's a hole,' said Horse, 'that'll be where the cobra appears from. They live in holes, don't they? See, I believe the purpose of this show, as Toon calls it, is to terrify the Enclave. Freeing the ants has left the shrews seriously disturbed. It's not just the loss of their records. It's the damage to their authority. They realize that once such a thing happens, it'll happen a second time and a third time . . . and soon, no one will pay the least attention to them. So – as I see it – they have to start a new campaign to re-establish their control over us mice. And maybe, in order to do that, they've found some way of teaming up with the snake.' She turned to Arvee. 'It sounds very unlikely, but that's how I see it, sir.'

Arvee said, 'An excellent analysis. Couldn't do better myself.'

Shane turned to Horse, 'OK, let's assume you're right and the snake makes an appearance tonight. What then? How will it change anything? The mice in the Enclave are already terrified out of their wits. Showing them the snake on a stage won't make much of a difference.'

'We don't know what the shrews have planned,' said Ellie. 'But it must be pretty fancy. They've got strips of reflective mirror-stuff hanging from the bushes and everything.'

'Right,' said Arvee. 'We'll only know for sure tonight.' He seemed preoccupied, looking frequently off into the distance. He kept smoothing back his whiskers. The other mice, watching him, caught his tension. But he didn't tell them what was worrying him.

'What about the cobra itself?' asked Shane. 'Are we going ahead with the plan we discussed for getting rid of it?'

'Well,' said Zero, glancing towards Arvee, 'we've taken the first step.' Arvee said nothing. 'Feather and Sparx went out about half an hour ago. They'll report back to us very soon now, I expect.' Then she broke off to address Arvee directly. 'Arvee, I realize you're disappointed with us. But as a compromise between taking action against the snake ourselves and doing nothing to defend ourselves, I believe the plan has great merit. I wish you felt the same as the rest of us do about this!'

Arvee's ears drooped. He said, in a quiet voice, 'I wish I did too, Zero. I really do. But I can't.' There was a heavy silence. 'There has to be a better way of solving problems than just *destroying* them! That's the human way. Not the animal way.' He shrugged. 'But I still don't have any practical ideas. So – yes – Feather and Sparx have gone out to call in "Hunter" Bangle, the local mongoose. For everyone's sake, I hope they come back soon and safe. I hope this situation ends in a way that makes the largest number of mice happy.' But he sighed heavily as he said it.

Then he continued, 'I suppose you're all wondering why I've been quiet. Well, I won't hide it any more. It's because none of us has seen or heard anything of my house guest, Cutie. I think we must assume she's fallen victim to the snake. There's no other explanation for her continued absence. It's going to be very difficult for me to explain this to Mo, my young human friend. She'll blame herself for being careless about safety, security and so on. This in turn will very likely result in my movements in and out of the house being restricted even further than they are already.

'I think all of you know how much it means to me to be able to meet you. It saddens me beyond words to recognize that I can't invite all of you into my life and my home. It reminds me of all the ways in which I am imprisoned. Not quite like the residents of Lantana Enclave, but. . . when it comes to crucial freedoms, I'm in a trap from which I can't escape without breaking a little girl's heart. Freedom is a very strange thing. It's as precious as life itself, and yet the only time we become aware of it is when we no longer have it.'

21

SHOWTIME!

Sunday Night

Ever since getting dressed, Cutie had been either angry, uncomfortable or scared. Speaking to Pasha made her angry, because he *refused* to see that she was a performer in her own right and that she deserved to have a say on the evening of her opening night. Every time she tried to improvise the speech he'd got her to memorize, he lost his temper and shouted at her.

Then, when it was finally time to get going, she was told that she would be seated on an upturned sugar bowl, which would be strapped down on to Stinky-Poo's head.

She and the snake were to travel up a leaf-filled passage. She had to hold a hot, flimsy plastic sheath of bubble wrap over herself to protect her from the leaves, until the final moment of emergence. 'That's ridiculous!' she squeaked at Pasha. 'No performer can be given instructions of this sort at the last minute! I must rehearse – I must be sure that I can get the timing right.'

But Pasha was immovable. 'You'll do it my way or not at all,' he said.

'You can't treat me like this – you *need* me!'

Pasha bent down till his huge dark head was close to hers. His large eyes, filmed over with their ghastly milky whiteness, peered into her face. His long black whiskers bristled all round her head. 'Listen to me, my little freak-fur princess,' he said in his ugliest voice, 'and listen well. I am delighted that you dropped in to my parlour. Your help could be an invaluable part of my larger scheme. But the moment you become more trouble to me than I can afford, I'll discard you and return to Plan "A" – the one I had before you appeared. I'll send up one of my faithful little mute mice, paint her white, dress her as you're dressed and, instead of letting her speak – since she can't – I'll speak for her instead. And you know what?' He frowned as if wondering whether to do this anyway, 'I bet I'd do a better job than you.'

He straightened up. 'Your accent is all wrong for a start. Some of the mice might not understand you. And the fact that you're a real albino might be too much for the faint-hearted among them.' He seemed almost to be talking to himself as he began to pace up and down in the confined space of Cutie's room. 'Yes, yes – it may be a better idea all around to go to Plan "A" right away, rather than risk letting you mess things up for me.'

That was when Cutie began to feel afraid. She couldn't be sure he wasn't fooling. Even though it was almost time for the show to start, she knew that he could and *would* cancel her performance if he decided he would be better off that way. She knew that she was snack-meat from the moment she couldn't prove her worth to him. Swallowing her pride, she backtracked all the way, begging to be allowed to do all the things she had earlier refused to consider.

She was pinning all her hopes on the possibility that, at some point in the evening's programme, *if* Arvee did come, she might be able to signal to him to say that she needed rescuing. And even if he didn't come, perhaps Toon might turn up. She already knew he was good at being a rescuer. But if Pasha didn't let her perform at all, she'd lose her only chance to make contact with the outside world.

Pasha had warned her, however, that he would be lurking above ground, hidden in the shadows behind the stage. She knew that it might be impossible to separate herself from Stinky-Poo. And even if she did, Pasha would very likely ensure that the snake hunted her down at once. The more she thought about the situation, the more she realized that, even with all her brains, her beauty and her Laboratory training, she might be unable to do anything at all to help herself.

So when the time came for Cutie to ascend her silver throne, it was with trembling whiskers and tears threatening to spill from her eyes. The mute mouse attendants tried to reassure her as much as they could. She and they had grown quite friendly. They showed her that they'd not been born mute after all. Instead they'd had their tongues cut out as punishment, in the bad old days of Ratland, when they'd been caught as young mouse rebels. Through mime and sign language they indicated to her that they feared and hated Pasha. However, they were equally afraid that other mice would reject them for having worked for the Ratlord. So they had remained in his service, sad and unwilling, the last remnants of his evil rule.

Cutie's robe was fastened down on to the bowl with termite glue in such a way that she'd rip it if she fell or tried to jump free. Once Cutie was secured, Stinky-Poo was summoned. He lay with his head flat on the ground. A strap was passed through perforations in the rim of sugar bowl, then round the snake's head. Stinky-Poo's sickening stench enveloped Cutie.

Finally, it was time to go.

Slowly at first, then with gathering speed, the strange pair began to move forward. Cutie knew that Pasha sat astride the snake's head when they went out on hunting raids. She had wondered what that felt like. Now she knew: it was like sitting above a solid river of flowing muscle. The sugar bowl swayed this way and that, rocked by the motion of the snake. Cutie could feel the surging power of the creature beneath her and the way the scales of its belly rippled forward, finding purchase on the uneven floor of the tunnel created by shrew engineers. There were no glow-worms to light their way. In the darkness, and with the heat under the plastic cover, the fetid smell of the snake and the swirling motion beneath her, Cutie was terrified that she might throw up.

Fortunately, the journey was not a long one. At the end of the tunnel, where the passage took a sharp turn upward, Stinky-Poo stopped and began to tuck the rest of his long body in coils beneath his head. In the pitch darkness, Cutie could hear the rustling of leaves, then felt them surrounding her, as the slowly compacting coils caused the snake's head to rise up inside the vertical passage. It was an unpleasant, suffocating sensation, to be surrounded by the dry, shifting weight of the leaves. She was glad, now, of the protection of the bubble plastic that she held over her.

22

YOW-WOW-WOW!

Sunday Night

Feather and Sparx crept slowly and carefully along the outside of the boundary wall of Paradise Villa. They had brought Arvee's bicycle with them, having been taught how to ride that afternoon. But the luxuriant growth of grass on the other side of the wall made riding difficult, so they were wheeling it along. The wall followed the course of an old storm-water drain, now overgrown with weeds. On the other side of the drain was a cement pavement. Three cement sewerage pipes bridged the drain, providing crossing points from the boundary wall to the pavement.

'I've never been outside the garden before!' whispered Feather to Sparx. 'Have you?'

'A couple of times,' said Sparx, hoping he sounded tougher than he felt.

It was late at night and there were very few cars on the road. The moon had risen high enough that it was visible above the tops of the trees around them. Apart from the sounds of nocturnal natural life, all was quiet.

'We're coming up towards the second cement pipe now. It's the one after this that we cross, right?'

'That's what the squirrels told us,' said Feather. 'I'm never very sure how much we can trust them. They always seem a little snooty and superior. Too bad we can't ask these ants directly for information!'

She was referring to the ants clinging to her shoulders and sitting on her head. Ever since the rescue in the Record Room, she had found herself being mobbed by small groups of the little creatures. They didn't share a language with her and they didn't get in her way. Nevertheless, there were now always a few close to her. She didn't especially like the constant attention, but she didn't want to hurt their feelings by brushing them off. She guessed it was their way of showing appreciation for having been rescued.

'We'd go faster if we took the paved path and rode the cycle,' said Sparx.

'We'll do that on the way back,' said Feather. 'We'll wheel the bike over the pipe, and leave it on the other side of the drainage ditch. That way, when we're leaving, we can just hop on it and ride off.'

Sparx agreed. Neither of them voiced the fear that they might have to leave in a hurry.

They crossed the pipe and continued walking in the prescribed direction. Soon they were standing beside an old banyan tree whose branches spread high above and on either side of the paved path. In the way of banyan trees, it had started to colonize the patch of road on which it stood, sending down aerial roots from above, while pushing up the cement paving slabs round its base from below.

The mice placed their bike just beside the nearest paving stones, but hidden by a clump of weeds. Looking around, they soon saw a broken plate half-buried in the soil between the cement pavement and the tree. This, the squirrels had said, pointed directly towards the entrance of the Bangle residence, which was a hole in the ground.

Feather shone her torch around. 'There!' she whispered to Sparx. 'I see it.'

The hole had been disguised to look like a shadow beneath one root of the tree. If not for the squirrels' instructions, the mice would never have found it.

'Is there some special way of calling him?' Sparx asked.

Feather shook her head. If there was, she didn't know it.

Both mice stood at the entrance to the den, not wanting to go in.

'It seemed like a great idea to ask for the mongoose's help back at the neem tree,' whispered Sparx. 'But now that we're here, I'm not so sure!'

'The squirrels laughed when I told them why I wanted to know his address. They said he's old and cranky. That he'd eat us sooner than talk to us. And that he'll only work for humans. Belongs to one of the old families, they said, related on his mother's side to the original Rikki-Tikki-Tavi –'

'Who?'

'Search me!' giggled Feather softly. 'Must be some famous mongoose –'

A low, breathy and somewhat slurred voice spoke up then from deep inside the burrow. 'Illiterate foo'sh – *hic!* – never heard of – *hic!* – Rudyard Kipling? *Hic!*' it said, giving both mice a bad shock. 'Giddy creatures! Dishturbing my – *hic!* – resht! Get away from my entrance – *hic!* – if you don't want to become my midnight shnack, that is! *Hic!*'

Sparx and Feather sprang back and wriggled under a broken cement slab. 'Oh – Mr Bangle, sir,' squeaked Feather, 'please – if you would be so kind –'

'Don't be – *hic!* – nonshenshical!' growled the mongoose. 'The only way – *hic!* – a mongoosh can be kind to a mouse – *hic!* – is by shnapping its neck quickly! Now, GO!'

Sparx whispered urgently to Feather, 'I think he's drunk! In which case he'd never be able to catch the snake, even if he wanted to.'

There came the sounds of an animal scrabbling up to its own front entrance. A moment later the fierce, pointed snout of a mongoose poked out from the hole. His bold red eyes flashed in the light of the just-risen moon. 'Drunk I may be,' he snarled, 'but not – *hic!* – deaf! Now –' he swung his head this way and that – 'where are you? If you're so deshperate to become part of my diet, the leasht you can do is to be visible . . .' He came out of the hole, a long lithe animal, grey in colour, with darker bands from his narrow head to the end of his long thin tail.

Feather and Sparx had wedged themselves tight under their cement slab. 'We're not coming out unless you promise not to eat us,' said Feather. Even as the words came out of her mouth, however, she had to admit they sounded foolish. There's no point making deals with predators!

Sniff-sniff-sniff-hic! went Mr Bangle's eager, questing nose. *Sniff-sniff-sniff-hic!* He located the mice instantly. But he couldn't quite get under the cement slab. Turning his head so that he could look at them, he said, 'Aha! I shee you! Now why don't – *hic!* – you jush come out, like good – but mad – little mice – *hic!* shtraight into my waiting jaws?'

'Excuse me,' said Feather, doing her best to sound very prim, 'but we've come to ask for your professional

help. If you can give it to us, well and good. If not –
goodnight!'

'Brave wordsh – *hic!* – my giddy little friendsh. But
they won't – *hic!* – save you. You woke me up – *hic!* and
now you'll pay the price!' With his paws, he began to
scrabble at the earth under the pavement.

Sparx and Feather squeezed themselves as far back
as they could go, then Sparx yelled, 'Mr Bangle, there's
a young cobra in our garden! If you follow us, you'll
have a much better meal than we'll provide!'

Mr Bangle chuckled. It was a curious sound, something
between a cackle and a rattle. 'He-he-he-heh! Oh, my
friendsh – *hic!* – isn't it clear that my hunting daysh –
hic! – are over? To fight a cobra takesh shpeed – *hic!* –
and brains and agility – *hic!* – and I am losing all three
– *hic!* – Sho forget it, OK? Don't talk to me about – *hic!* –
shnakes and I'll not tell anyone that you offered your
shweet little – *hic!* – shelves to me without sho much
as an – *hic!* – invitation!'

The claws of his small, strong paws raked the earth
under the pavement again and again. With a despairing
squeak, Feather felt herself beginning to slide down, as
the loose dirt gave way in front of her. But Sparx grabbed
her and held her tight. 'Don't worry,' he whispered into
her ear. 'I won't let you fall –'

'What'sh the matter – *hic!* – little shquirts?' called
the mongoose. 'Losht your nerve?' He stuck his narrow

snout into the space he had created. His alcohol-scented breath was right in Feather's face and she could see his small white teeth grinning at her in the darkness. It was too much for her and she shut her eyes.

'Come out – *hic!* – foolish moushies, come to Bangle!' His voice boomed weirdly under the slab. 'Time for dinner . . . oh!' He stopped suddenly.

'OUCH! Yow! ' he exclaimed. With a yelp that was deafening at such close quarters, he shot back. 'Ow! Eek! Yow – *Wowowowowow!* Stop it – stop! Yow!'

The two mice, who had both felt their last moment was at paw, were frozen with fear. Sparx recovered first. He didn't understand why, or how, but they'd been given a reprieve. No doubt it would be brief. 'Come on, quick!' he said in Feather's ear. 'Let's make a dash for the bicycle!'

'But he's still out there!' squeaked Feather. 'This might just be a trick to get us to come out!'

Sparx pushed her forward so that she had no choice but to roll down the dip created by the mongoose's digging. 'He was about to catch us anyway, so he didn't need to bother with tricking us – go, go, go! This way!'

Half-pushing, half-pulling her, he scrambled out from under the cement slab. The broken plate lay to their right. Both mice sprang towards it, plunged into the clump of weeds, then out again, towards the pavement. There was the trusty bicycle, still standing where they had left it. Sparx leaped on the driver's seat, while Feather hopped on behind him. Together they tore off down the footpath as fast as Sparx's feet could pedal.

Behind them, they could hear the mongoose's cries of pain and bewilderment as he thrashed about in the grass at the base of the tree, snorting and spitting. '*Owww!* OW! Gerroff me – Wha'sh got into you ants? *YOW-OW-OW!* That was inside my NOSE! My EARS! YOW-WOW-WOW!'

The two mice were practically back at the front gate of Paradise Villa before Sparx slowed to a halt. He was puffing and panting and blowing his cheeks out with the effort.

'Whooo! Oh-ho-ho!' huffed Sparx. 'Oh, my! I thought we were cooked for sure!'

'Me too,' said Feather, 'I forgot I had ants sitting on me! How clever – and brave – of them to go and bite him.'

'We'd better get back to the neem tree as soon as possible. The others must be wondering what happened to us.'

Feather looked up. 'The moon's right overhead. You know what that means?'

'Never mind!' urged Sparx. 'We can't afford to be standing out in the middle of a paved pathway on a moonlit night! The grass is thinner here. We'll be able to take the cycle under the front gate.'

The two mice set off again, this time with Feather riding the cycle. 'Somehow,' she said, over her shoulder, 'I'm not so unhappy that our mission has failed.'

'That's because it *couldn't* have succeeded,' said Sparx. 'It was a plan that didn't take into account the fact that mongooses eat mice, even crazy old Mr Bangle. So we'll just have to think of another plan, that's all.'

'I've had quite enough of plans for one night,' said Feather, as she turned in towards the front gate. 'We're lucky to have survived this one!'

They passed under the wrought-iron gate, then took a sharp right again under the potted ferns that rimmed the driveway. The earth was bare there. Up ahead was the first of the euphorbia pots that marked the boundary of Lantana Enclave.

'Do you hear something?' asked Sparx.

'Must be the show,' answered Feather, 'the one that the shrews were busy arranging. It was due to begin with the moon directly overhead. Quick – if we hurry, we might just catch it!'

23

THE PLATFORM OF TRUTH

Sunday Midnight

As the moon rose higher, so did the level of excitement in Lantana Enclave. What with the curfews and the fears of sudden attack, the mice had few opportunities to be out of their homes. The regular public meetings, which everyone was obliged to attend, were dreary affairs. But this gathering, so it was rumoured, was going to be different.

'The snake's going to address us directly!' said the more fearful of the colony's residents. 'It's going to tell us to stop resisting our fate! To lie down and accept being swallowed!'

'Nonsense,' said others. 'It's the exact opposite. The leader of the shrews is going to address us directly, to say that he's sent the snake packing.'

'No! It's going to be completely different from anything we can imagine,' said yet others. 'Something that'll help us fight. Something that'll tell us why terrible things have been happening to us.'

No one could understand why the shrews were being so mysterious. Then again, they were getting used to being treated as if they didn't deserve to know more than they were told. 'It's good for us,' they said to one another. 'We don't have the experience or the discipline to survive in the garden. The shrews have been living here for centuries. We have no choice but to wait for them to tell us what to do.'

As the moment for the show to start drew near, residents began coming out of their homes, moving to the clearing in the centre of the colony. They were dressed in the drab clothes required of them in public, with their heads covered. Tails had to be kept under tight control, either tucked completely out of sight or restrained in pouches. Yet, despite it all, there was an air of celebration coursing through the Enclave.

The shrews were directing the flow of spectators, shouting orders, pushing the mice around. Privately, though, there were fears about the anticipated event among them too. It was said that Officer Diss had suffered a nervous collapse. His wife had taken over the running of the show. One of his sub-inspectors had vanished.

No one knew whom to believe or what to think.

Officer Diss swallowed a handful of camomile seeds to calm himself down. He'd been swallowing camomile seeds ever since his last encounter with Pasha, but it had still taken him a full day to recover from the trauma of watching one of his officers disappearing down the throat of the snake. He was standing beside the clearing. Overhead, the moon was shining bright. From all around came the murmur of conversation and rustling movements as the massed mice stood under the branches of the two lantana bushes closest to the clearing.

Diss held a field cricket in his paws. It had been muffled all this while. Now he raised it high and removed the string that prevented its back legs from moving. Immediately its raucous stridulation rent the air: *reeEEECH-i-reeEEECH-i-reeEEECH-i!* This was the signal for silence. Only Diss knew that, inside the leaf-filled passage behind him, Cutie would also hear the cricket and signal Stinky-Poo to begin his ascent.

The mice quietened down. Diss handed the cricket to Dwindle, who was standing close by. The sub-inspector bit off the insect's head gladly. One of the perks of acting as Diss's attendant at public meetings was being handed the attention-cricket. The stridulation stopped abruptly.

'Residents of Lantana Enclave!' began Officer Diss. 'You are about to witness a sight seen by none before you! I ask you to direct your attention to the spot behind me. It will be known from now on as the Platform of Truth.'

He paused to clear his throat. He had a recorder ant concealed under the collar of his jacket to prompt him with keywords for his speech. The ant seemed to have got stuck on the word 'truth' and was repeating monotonously, '-ruth, -ruth, -ruth'. Diss tweaked its antenna. It jerked forward to the next word: 'purpose'.

'Ah – uh – the purpose of this . . . this platform will be made clear by the end of this evening. At the end of it, you will have no . . . uh . . . uh . . . questions or doubts. You will become Believers. You will become Acceptors.'

'-tors, -tors, -tors,' said the ant in its mechanical voice. Diss gave it another tweak. He could hear a rustling of the leaves in the pit behind him. He knew this meant that Stinky-Poo was about to appear.

'Ah – some of you have expressed unhappiness with the solutions we shrews have evolved for living in the garden. We knew that you mice did not have the intelligence or understanding to follow our methods. Nevertheless, we did our best to . . . uh . . . uh . . . educate you. To pull you up to our high standards.

'However, the act of vandalism in the Neighbourhood Security Office was an indication that our best efforts have been a waste. Our precious records were utterly destroyed.

'We were ready to give up. We were ready to go back to the kitchen garden and leave you mice defenceless against the forces of nature. But then a miracle happened. A White Mouse appeared from nowhere. She has joined forces with th-th-the S-s-snake. She says that you mice must be given one last chance to straighten yourselves up and become better residents of Lantana Enclave.' Diss could hear the rustling behind him growing louder. He began to panic. He didn't trust himself to remain composed once the serpent appeared.

'Y-you m-m-mice – uh – uh – must be g-g-g-g – uhh given One Lunch Order!' he said, getting his words and phrases badly mixed up. 'To . . . to . . . Straighten Cups and . . . and become . . . uh . . . uh . . . Butter Restaurants of Lantern Ankle!' The rustling was growing louder by the second. 'And . . . uh . . . uh . . . in Conk . . . onk-oink-oink . . . Conclusion, I repeak – repark – recork – uh . . . *EEEeekk!*'

From the space behind him, a leaf had drifted down and touched the officer's hind legs. It instantly brought to mind the snake's flickering tongue. Diss dropped forward in a dead faint.

But even as his shriek faded away, a low, wondering moan was issuing from the throats of all the watching mice and shrews. They no longer had eyes or ears for Diss. Their gaze was rooted to the spot behind the Neighbourhood Security Officer. Boiling up out of the ground, under a veritable spout of softly rustling dead leaves, came an apparition in pure white.

It had the shape and size of a mouse, but apart from that it looked like nothing the awestruck residents of Lantana Enclave had ever seen. Its fur and hair were silvery white. Its outspread ears were like angel wings. It wore a robe that shimmered and twinkled in the moonlight, as if a living star had fallen out of the sky. It sat upon a silver throne. Their hearts and minds were filled with reverence.

Alone amidst all the gathered assembly, three mice knew immediately who and what they were looking at. 'Oh, no!' gasped Toon, Ellie and Arvee, under their breath. 'It's . . . Cutie!'

24

CRAZIER THAN CUTIE

Sunday Midnight

At the moment when the leaves parted above Cutie, she rose into the glorious moonlight, dropping her arms and the plastic cover instinctively. Her ears and whiskers were spread wide with the sheer delight of being in the open again. The night air was so fresh after the smelly, stuffy confines of Pasha's lair that she wanted to throw her head back and drink it in in great gulps. All of this added tremendously to the impact she had on the throng of Lantana Enclave's mice. They watched with mouths agape as the vision in white opened her arms wide and threw her head back, appearing to beam with indescribable joy.

The moment didn't last.

Cutie counted one-two-three-four-five seconds. Then she tapped her foot on Stinky-Poo's head. He understood the signal. Once more, he began to rise. This time, his own head began to emerge from the pit, as he bore the mouse up . . . up . . . up . . .

High into the bright moonlight, the young snake raised his head. His black scales glistened, his pale throat blazed, his gracefully curved hood was fully extended and his whole dark gleaming body swayed. His tongue flickered out between his curved white fangs and his mouth opened as he hissed out his challenge and his warning. Like a crystal crown above his head, the fragile figure of the white mouse sparkled and shone.

It was a vision that was at once terrifying and beautiful, bizarre and wonderful.

Among the mice, breathless wonder turned into whimpering fear.

Cutie felt light-headed with power as she swayed high above the crowd. It was all happening exactly as Pasha had said it would. She began her prepared speech.

'Residents of Lantana Enclave . . . hear my words and tremble!

'I . . . am the Spirit of the Garden!'

Cutie wished she could shade her eyes. The moonlight was too dazzling after her time underground. She could barely see her audience and those she could see appeared to be drab and ill-dressed. Not at all the kind of audience she would expect for her glittering debut as a major entertainer! Nevertheless, she had to continue.

'I am the Light and the Darkness.

'What I ask of you, you shall give.

'What I give to you, you shall accept.

'What I say to you, you shall believe . . .'

Cutie blinked and blinked. There was only one face she yearned to see and that was Arvee's. Saving which, she wouldn't have minded seeing Toon's face either. She hadn't forgotten the chivalrous manner in which he had rescued her when she fell off the windowsill. But instead, all she saw were countless, unrecognizable house mice staring at her with their mouths open.

And in the great distance, confusingly, she heard what might have been, in any other context, the sound of bicycle tyres on dry leaves. Of course, that was impossible. None of the mice in the garden had a bicycle.

Meanwhile, she had to continue!

'I am the Answer and the Question.

'Those who believe in me shall have no Questions.

'But those who question me shall receive no Answers . . .'

One by one, the small figures in the crowd were beginning to kneel down in front of Cutie. They were holding their arms crossed over their heads in such a way that their eyes were completely covered, their paws raised and helpless. No one was clapping or cheering. No one was even looking at her any more. Cutie felt keen disappointment. It seemed that the house mice had no appreciation of her acting skills or her delivery.

She came to the final part of her speech.

'In the months ahead, I will visit you from time to time.

'In return, you will obey my servants, the shrews.

'Those who do not will face my wrath.

'And suffer the consequences.

'This is all for today.'

Cutie tapped her foot on Stinky-Poo's head. Immediately, he began to sink down.

'I shall leave you now.

'Go in peace.

'Go in silence.

'Await my return.'

With that, Cutie began once more to vanish into the pile of leaves. Officer Diss had finally recovered from his swoon. He deployed his sub-inspectors to raise a screen of ferns around the spot so that the exact details of Stinky-Poo's disappearance could not be witnessed by the audience. But no one among the gathered mice and shrews was looking. They remained in their positions of terrified reverence long after the rustling from the Platform of Truth had ceased. The Neem Tree Gang didn't shut their eyes, but they were also compelled to kneel, in order to avoid detection.

The shrews waited a full two minutes for the sounds of rustling leaves to die away before giving the all-clear.

Officer Diss spoke: 'Residents of Lantana Mouse Enclave, you may now disperse. Move slowly and keep your silence. Remain in your homes till further notice. Details of the next public meeting will be released to you via shrews bearing recorder ants. Trust no one and nothing unless it is a shrew.'

The presentation was over.

Back in the Web Room, Zero's team regrouped around Feather and Sparx. The tale of their narrow escape left all the mice feeling breathless.

Zero turned to Arvee. 'You were right,' she said, wanting to be fair. 'You warned us against approaching the mongoose.'

Arvee thanked her for her friendly gesture. 'Meanwhile, what can we do about Cutie?' he said. 'I'm very relieved to know she's alive, but. . . I can't imagine how or why she's allowed herself to be used by the shrews in this way.'

'How do you know she's being used?' Crax asked. 'Maybe she believes in what she's doing. Maybe she's gone a little mad – got lost in the undergrowth, met the shrews and . . .'

'No!' said Ellie. 'I've spoken with her. She's not mad at all. But she might be a bit confused.'

'A *bit*?' exclaimed Bizzy. 'I'd say she's as dizzy as a moth in sunlight! I mean, a mouse that sits on the head of a snake has already lost its whiskers in my opinion! Quite apart from all that nonsense she was spouting.'

'Well, yes,' said Arvee, 'except that it doesn't add up. Cutie's vain and she behaves as if she's empty-headed, but those lines today were just not characteristic of her. It's like Zero keeps saying – there's something else going on here, something very obvious that we're not seeing for what it really is.' He shook his head. 'Meanwhile, now that we know where she is, I don't think we have a choice – we've got to get her away from there.' He looked around at the others. 'And there's only one way I can think of doing it.'

'No, Arvee, no!' said Zero. 'You're *not* going in all by yourself. It would only result in each of us going in after you to save you, one at a time, until there's no one left to save!' She was smiling as she spoke, but at the same time, it was clear that she meant what she said. 'Cutie's our problem too now, not just yours. So don't feel responsible and apologetic for using our resources to find your house guest. Your fate is our fate, remember?'

The other mice clapped and cheered.

'Oh, but I'm uniquely equipped to deal with the situation,' said Arvee earnestly. 'Think about it. After the appearance of the Spirit of the Garden tonight, it's not going to be enough to just stop her from appearing again. You saw how the mice behaved – completely intimidated. The shrews are back in control and the snake is still at large. We have to reverse the influence of the Spirit at once, right away, or else we're back where we began.'

'All right,' said Zero, frowning, 'but I don't see why that involves you in any unique way.'

'I do!' said Ellie, jumping to her feet. 'I know what you're thinking, Arvee. You're a white mouse and so you think you can go down there, dress up as Cutie, climb on the snake and deliver your *own* kind of message'

'Why, yes!' said Arvee, looking very surprised. 'How *did* you guess? I thought it was very clever of me to think of it.'

'Oh! You're even *more* crazy than Cutie, in that case!' exclaimed Ellie. 'What makes you imagine you can get way with that kind of deception? How does she get herself on and off the snake? And what if the snake guesses you're not her, what then?'

'Ah,' said Arvee, grinning. 'It won't guess! I've worked it out, you see. There're two reasons why I feel I can get away with it. One is that Cutie wears perfume, which disguises her own real smell. I bet she was wearing some when she went away, because she's never without it. The other reason is the *snake* has a smell! *We* all know that – it was something that struck me at the time of that first encounter out in the grass.

I mean, it's one of the things that's been puzzling me. A snake has to be able to sneak up on its prey. But this one's got a knockout stink, which probably warns prey for miles around that there's something big and bad approaching. The chances are, it doesn't ever manage to catch anything on its own –'

Horse was nodding her head, 'I see where you're going with this, Arvee. You're saying it's not just by chance that the snake's been terrorizing Lantana. It's been brought there, by the shrews, *because* it can't catch anything on its own.'

'Well, OK,' said Toon, 'except. . . do any of you see the shrews working this out for themselves? I don't. They don't have that kind of imagination. Nor does the snake, I'll bet. It's big and dangerous, sure. But I was looking at it tonight – I mean really looking at it, and how often does any one of us get a chance to do that, right? – and it seemed to me that it looked a bit dim.'

'I think you're right, Toon,' said Arvee. 'Something about it was juvenile!'

'This is crazy!' remarked Zero. 'Are you suggesting the snake's allowed itself to be pushed around by a bunch of shrews? There can't be many snakes in existence that would get themselves into such a situation.'

'We're all being distracted,' said Ellie. 'Let's get back to where we started – with Arvee dressing up as Cutie –'

So Arvee explained to the others about the day he had spent impersonating his house guest.

'All right,' said Zero, 'you've had one day's rehearsal. But what's to say that Ellie – or I – or any other mouse wouldn't do just as well as you, so long as we bleached our fur white?' This was something that had already been successfully tried out, the previous year, when Ellie had impersonated Arvee at the time of the Ratland Rebellion.

Arvee twiddled his ears. 'It's just this thing, you see,' he said. 'There's a piece missing from the puzzle and if we could only see what it was, all the others would fall into place. But without this piece, I can only tell you what I know deep in my whiskers: if I don't go myself, the plan won't work at all.'

'In that case,' said Ellie, 'I have to say that I know, deep in *my* whiskers, that if I don't come along, the plan won't work either! I mean – it's not really a plan at all! So far, all you've told us is that you expect to run in and rescue Cutie from under the nose of a cobra – then leave yourself in her place.' She looked around at the others for support. 'It's not adding up.'

Cocky, one of the younger mice, put up her hand. 'You've still not addressed the problem of the snake,' she said. 'How it's going to be got rid of now that the mongoose won't help us. Or have I missed something?'

'You're absolutely right,' said Arvee. He sighed deeply now, smoothing back his whiskers. 'There's one solution I can think of and it would certainly work. But it's harsh medicine.'

He looked around at his friends. The bleak expression had returned to his face. 'Cutie and I between us could, I think, explain to the humans that there's a cobra in the undergrowth.'

There was an immediate tightening of the atmosphere in the Web.

'Yes. I know exactly how you all feel about that, and you'd be right: it would mean the end of the garden as we know it. Mo's parents would tear this whole place up if they had the slightest idea there was a snake in there. They'd rip out the bougainvillea, dig up the lantanas and most probably shift the thorny plants away. It's what I feared would happen if Cutie never returned. And it could *still* happen, if we're not careful.'

'Just a minute –' began Ellie, 'if you are planning to take Cutie's place –'

Arvee was starting to tug on his whiskers in the way he had when he was exceptionally stressed. 'I know, I know – it means we have very little time! We've got to run into that place where Cutie appeared from, snatch her, subdue the snake, ride it back up the pit, address the mice, undo the effects of Cutie's speech – and get both of us back into *Mercara* without the humans knowing any of it!'

'I'm pleased to notice,' said Ellie, in what she hoped was a comforting way, 'that you said "we" . . .'

25

DISGUISES AND DECEPTIONS

Monday

Three mice – Arvee, Heavy and Willing – returned to *Mercara*. Arvee spent time with Mo, dressed alternately as himself and as Cutie. Meanwhile, the other two mice dusted their fur with talcum powder and took turns flitting about inside the doll's house. They made sure that only one of them was ever in view and they tried not to squeak or run when the little girl approached the table. 'Remember,' Arvee said to them, 'she's used to thinking of us as her best friends. If either of you shows the slightest sign of nervousness, she'll be hurt and worried.' The situation wasn't supposed to last for more than one day, after which, Arvee hoped, it would no longer be necessary to deceive his human friend.

In this way, they managed to maintain the illusion that both Mo's pets were safely in residence. All three slept soundly during the time that Mo was away at school, in order to be well rested for the night. At ten o'clock Arvee made cracker-pizzas for the three of them. He smothered three crackers in pasta sauce, covered each one with slices of pepperoni and olive, topped them with grated Parmesan and then grilled them one at a time in a little electric oven he'd improvised for himself from the heating coil of a hair-dryer.

'Ooh!' groaned Willing, 'I've eaten too much! It'll take two Mantis Airline flights to get me to the tree!'

'You deserve it,' said Arvee warmly. 'You did a great job today, masquerading as Cutie and me.'

'That was yummy!' said Heavy. 'I could easily eat another two. Too bad we've got to go off tonight.'

'Well, you'll just have to come back,' said Arvee, 'when this business is over.'

A short while later, the mice were ready to leave. They climbed up to the windowsill and began blinking their torches to call up the mantises. Willing patted Arvee's backpack. 'What's *this?*' he asked. There was something big and bulky in there. 'It smells exactly like the pepperoni on our pizzas!'

'That's what it is,' said Arvee. 'Plus a remote-controlled toy car –' Just then, a flight came in to land with a loud buzzing clatter of insect wings, 'I'll have to tell you later!' yelled Arvee over the din.

By the time they reached the neem tree, however, there was no time for explanations. 'Whizzbang and Spud have been inside the Enclave,' said Toon, 'checking the site from which the snake appeared.'

'How did they get in?' Arvee wanted to know. 'There are so few mice out in the open, it must be difficult to get past the shrew sentries without being noticed.'

'They were disguised as snails!' said Toon, trying not to look too proud of himself. It had been his idea. 'Two huge snails, creeping along very slowly, checking everything out, before turning around and coming back to us. They said there are five shrews standing around the Platform of Truth, from where the snake and Cutie came up. According to them, it seems to be an ordinary pit, covered to the top with dead leaves. Shouldn't be impossible for the two of you to slip into it once you get past the shrews.'

'Where are the twins now?'

'They went back into the colony, as snails. Their plan was to get under a bush where no one will notice them and remove their shells. They should be in there now, waiting for you and Ellie to go in.'

'And what'll *we* be disguised as?' Arvee asked, with a half-smile in his whiskers. He guessed it was going to be something as ingenious as the snails!

'Well, we considered everything from stick insects to caterpillars,' said Ellie, 'but in the end decided that it would be best to take a little assistance from Whee and Hum . . .' She smiled, 'I bet you've never asked yourself what Whee and Hum can be taught to do!'

Arvee glanced at her, then at the beetles, who were clinging to the webbing near him. They were twiddling their antennae enthusiastically and kicking up their back legs in a funny way. He watched them for a few seconds before realizing what their actions reminded him of. 'Oh no,' he groaned. 'Please, don't tell me . . .' Ellie was nodding her head and grinning. 'You've trained them to pretend they're DUNG beetles?'

'It's certainly not what they do for a living, but they *can* roll a ball of dung if they have to – but don't worry!' she said, seeing the look of alarm on Arvee's face. 'We're not going to be rolled up in real dung! The idea is to create *fake* dung balls in which we'll be hiding. Then the beetles can just roll us all the way up to the pit and toss us in. That's what we've been busy with here all day, preparing hollow fake dung balls in which you and I can sit. We made them out of neem twigs and leaves, with the help of a couple of spiders and their sticky silk. . . C'mon! You'll be really impressed. They're at the base of the tree.'

Arvee protested all the way down, trying to find objections to the plan. 'Whee and Hum won't know where to go!' he said. 'And what if a *real* dung beetle comes along and wants to snatch us from them? What if we get lost and remain locked for ever inside a ball of fake dung?'

'You worry too much,' said Toon, waggling his ears. 'We trained the beetles to push the balls in a straight line under a particular lantana bush. That's where Whizzbang and Spud will be waiting. They'll redirect the beetles to the pit – and the two of you'll be pushed in!'

'It sounds worse than it is,' said Ellie. 'Really. We sent Whee and Hum in just now, before you got here, with ordinary mud balls. They flew back to us with little bits of coloured string attached to their back legs, a sign from Whizzbang and Spud to say that they did great. No one pays attention to insects except when they want to eat them. Fortunately for us, Whee and Hum aren't an edible species, so no one will give them a second glance.'

On the ground, Ellie showed Arvee the two big hollow spheres that had been prepared. From the outside, they looked very much like dark brown spheres of dung. But they had the sharp, bitter-sour scent of neem and they opened up rather like spherical hampers. They were quite spacious inside. 'There's a string to keep the two halves shut tight,' Ellie said, showing him, 'so we can't get locked in! And anyway, it's only leaves and bark. If anything goes very badly wrong, we can always poke holes in the sides and get out.'

Arvee looked as if he wanted nothing more than to be back in *Mercara*, curled up in bed. 'Ooo! I just *know* I'm not going to like this!' he said, looking nervous, embarrassed and amused all at once. Then he looked over at Ellie. 'But if you're game for it, Ellie, how can

I chicken out?' He gave her a big hug before throwing his backpack into the hollow sphere. Then he stepped gingerly into his cramped capsule. 'We'll have to work out our strategy once we're inside the pit. See you there!'

'Yes,' said Ellie as she got into her container. 'Good luck to you and to me!'

'Good luck!' called Zero from above. 'Safe journey!' Arvee looked up at the twinkling lights of the glow-worm landing strip. In the darkness, they were all he could see. Then Toon brought the lid down over him. Arvee knotted the string, securing the two halves shut from inside. Clutching his backpack to his chest, he wondered when next he would return above ground.

Five shrews were slumped at their posts in the moonlight. They had given up even pretending to guard the Platform of Truth. They had initially held fern fronds aloft, as pikes, but these had long since wilted and been abandoned. Sneak was lying, curled up, asleep on the ground. The other four were sitting on pebbles they had rolled close to the edge of the leaf-filled pit.

'Oi!' said Dwindle in a drowsy voice. 'You still awake?'

Furtive replied, with his eyes shut, ''Course. How 'bout you?'

Dwindle had to think about this for a few seconds before answering, 'No.'

Callous said, mumbling, 'Know? Know wot?'

Turgid, who was the only one sitting semi-upright, said, 'Know it all.'

'Eh?' responded Dwindle. 'Woz dat?'

'Nutting,' said Turgid, letting loose a little snore.

'Lawnmower,' said Sneak, in his sleep.

'Eh?' said Dwindle.

'Thez a lawnmower coming to geddus,' said Sneak.

'Wake up,' said Dwindle. 'S'time to sleep.'

Whizzbang and Spud had been sitting under a nearby bush with their noses buried deep in their paws to stop themselves from guffawing out loud as they listened to this thread of drowsy conversation. They took turns looking around until one of them caught sight of Whee and Hum. The two beetles were kicking two enormous balls of what looked very much like dung with their back legs, moving slowly and laboriously towards the twins.

This set the two young mice off snuffling with laughter again. It was a hilarious sight. Real dung beetles can rattle across great distances in a funny backwards position, with their heads down and pushing huge balls of dung with their back legs. Whee and Hum, poor things, were utterly unfamiliar with the technique. Sometimes they lost their grip and were left for several seconds with their multijointed legs waving about helplessly in the air. Sometimes they slipped sideways. Sometimes they flipped over. Sometimes they even found themselves rolling under the large, unwieldy balls.

By the time the two beetles drew level, Whizzbang and Spud were quite weak with suppressed laughter. Nevertheless, they appreciated the insects' heroic effort. They stroked their antennae and petted the creatures behind their necks for a few seconds before gently turning them in the right direction for going towards the pit.

Bending down to the fake dung ball nearest to him, Whizzbang whispered, 'All well in there?'

There was a low moan from inside.

This inspired a fresh round of giggles from both mice.

Arvee groaned from inside, 'This has to be the worst and most uncomfortable way to travel. I'm feeling so green with motion sickness I could impersonate a plant. *Stop laughing,* you little monsters!'

But it was no use. The experience of hearing a big, round and expressionless ball scolding them was almost too much for the twins. 'Don't say anything more, please,' they gasped, 'or we'll collapse!'

26

DANDELiON WiNE

Monday Night

Cutie was lying on the mattress in her room, sobbing uncontrollably. She'd had only two thimbles of brackish water to drink in all the time since she'd returned from her performance twenty-four hours ago. She was weak from hunger and thirst, and demoralized because of her captivity.

There was a knock on the door.

'Go away!' she said. 'I won't agree, I *won't*!'

The door was opened anyway. Pasha came in. 'Dearie me,' he said. 'What's this? Our princess is refusing to see reason!' He snapped his fingers. Two of his mute attendants came forward and pulled Cutie into an upright position on the mattress. She was wearing her own clothes, with no robe over them. The boots had been removed. She felt unwashed and miserable, her whiskers a tangled mess, her ears drooping almost to her shoulders. She did not look up when Pasha addressed her.

'You might as well feed me to the snake right away,' she said. 'I don't care any more.'

'Interesting!' said Pasha. 'Even after a day without food and water, she resists my generous offer. I'm impressed – I thought princesses were more concerned about their own survival than that.'

'This *isn't* survival,' said Cutie. 'It's imprisonment. I *don't* want to spend the rest of my life underground! I *don't* want to be a celebrity to a garden of stupid old house mice who are too scared to even look at me! I want a hot shower. I want fresh, clean clothes. And I *don't* want to talk to you any more! You're NOT NICE.'

Pasha laughed, exposing his fearsome yellow incisors. 'Ah, my feather-brained freak! "Nice" is for dummies! Losers. Weaklings. And I am none of those things. I must be restored to my natural position as a ruler and leader. An example to other creatures. The head of a dynasty. And I was doing perfectly well. I had everything an animal could want, until your famous friend, the one and only Dr Arvee, came along. He changed everything for me. The thought of having my revenge is the one thing that's kept me alive in all these uncomfortable months since he destroyed my world. If he thought I would just crawl away to die in an unmarked ditch, he doesn't know much about what it means to be a proud, powerful, dominant animal!

'But *that's* his weakness, isn't it? He doesn't know what it's like to be a normal animal. He doesn't understand about power and violence, he doesn't understand that the natural world is a naaaasty place. Oh, yes. He's about to learn an important lesson. I'm going to be the one to teach it to him. And you're going to help me do it – whether you want to or not.'

Cutie heard this ranting speech with a sinking feeling in her very empty stomach. 'You can't force me,' she said stubbornly. 'I won't go out again and I won't say what you want me to say. So there.'

'Fine words,' said Pasha, 'but pointless in the context. You're no different from your boyfriend after all. Your experience of life, with all its frilly trimmings – plucked whiskers, painted claws – has taught you nothing about the fangs and talons of raw survival. I was just being kind when I invited you to continue playing your role. I don't need you any more. All the mice have seen and heard you. Meanwhile, you've established to your fiancé that you're alive. You've served your function.

'If you'd been smart, you'd have recognized that, with my backing, you could have lived out the rest of your life as a goddess. But –' he shrugged '– no matter. If you won't cooperate, I can have bits and pieces of you conveyed back to the big house – a finger, a portion of tail, an ear. Your ardent suitor will eventually be forced to come in person to collect what's left of you. And he *will*. His goody-goody personality guarantees it. That's what makes him weak – his principles, his delicacy! He can't stop himself from doing the "right thing".'

'In that case,' cried Cutie, 'you *do* need something from me – you need me to be alive! Or he won't come. Isn't that so? He's not stupid. He'll know better than to risk himself for a cold pelt.'

'Yes,' said Pasha. 'That's so.' He had a twisted smirk on his face.

'Well, then,' said Cutie virtuously, 'I'll kill myself.'

'Of course you will, my little albino jewel! But have you thought about how you'll accomplish this trifling task?'

'Why, I'll . . . I'll starve myself to death – and it won't take long, considering I've not eaten for a whole day! There won't be anything you can do about it. You can't force me to eat!'

'No, no, I wouldn't dream of it,' said Pasha. He gestured to an attendant. 'I have a much better idea. Anticipating that you might be inclined to tread the martyr's path, I had my helpers prepare some rare delicacies for you.' He half-turned, as one of the mute mice returned bearing a tray with a number of dainty dishes on it. Mouth-watering aromas filled the small room. 'Here we are. Stewed aphid . . . crispy cricket wings . . . roasted grasshopper thighs in dandelion wine . . . tender grass shoots soaked in honey . . .' He directed the tray be placed close to Cutie. 'Now, I'm going to leave you to stare at that little feast while appreciating the brilliant manner in which you've guaranteed that your paramour will experience a painful and humiliating death in my custody. After he comes to fetch you, that is.'

Cutie's stomach gave out a loud squawk as the scent of food smote her sensitive nostrils. Her eyes filled with fresh tears. How was it possible for anyone to be so cruel to her? 'I won't touch a bite,' she said, in a faltering voice, even as she devoured the food with her eyes. 'I can be strong.'

'That's right,' said Pasha soothingly as he left the room. 'You just keep telling yourself that – and in the meantime, you know where to find a snack if you need one.'

The shrews guarding the mouth of the pit stirred. Turgid, who was at that moment the most awake of the five, said, 'Errrm . . . woz dat?' He opened one of his eyes and looked over his left shoulder. The moon was directly above him and the scene was bathed in its bluish-white light. He saw nothing.

Dwindle, who was fast asleep, did not answer.

Sneak snored.

Furtive said, both eyes shut, 'Nutting.'

But Callous said, 'Wha? Wha'cha say?' He raised his head from his chest and looked around. 'Summing suspicious?'

Turgid looked over his right shoulder. 'Summing russling over dere.' He saw what looked like a large black beetle scuttle away. There was another one just ahead of it. 'Eeh . . . innit strange?'

'Wha? Wha?' said Callous nervously.

Turgid shut both eyes again and smacked his lips a couple of times. 'Thawt I seen two twitchers jus' now.'

Callous said, 'Yes – I seen 'em too. Black uns. Rattling off. Wha' of it? Dey're not da edible kind.'

'I thawt I seen da same two afore, is all,' said Turgid, trying to find a comfortable angle at which to rest his head down on his chest. 'Fussing about wid mud balls. Like dey was dung beetles or summing. Doing a bad job of it too.' He was almost asleep again.

'Dat's ridiclous,' said Callous, also preparing to settle back into sleep. 'Dey's no sech ting as dung beetles wot don' know how to be dung beetles. Must'a bin dreaming.' A thought struck him. 'An a silly dream it woz, eh-eh-eh-eh,' he laughed, in a sleepy, creaky way. 'Eh-eh-eh-eh.'

'Shut dat russling, yer termites,' grumbled Dwindle. 'Some of us is trying ta guard dis place.'

'Shh,' muttered Sneak. 'Some of us is trying to stay awake.'

27

THE SNAKE PIT

Monday Night

The two large, dark spheres entered the leaf-filled pit with a crumbly rustle, falling slowly. They bumped down the slope at the end of the pit, rolling until they came to a place where the earth levelled out.

After a long pause, very cautiously, one of the balls stirred. Ellie, whose ball was in front of Arvee's, opened hers first. She looked out of the thin slit, seeing nothing. Not the slightest glimmer of light showed in any direction. She poked her nose out and sniffed hard. The terrible stench of the serpent, though present, was not strong. Very slowly, she risked raising the lid of her fake dung ball higher. Turning her nose this way and that in the pitch darkness, she located Arvee's ball behind hers. 'Arvee!' she whispered. 'Are you all right?'

There was a groan from inside the leaf-and-bark sphere. 'Ooarrgghhh,' he whispered back. 'That's something I never want to do again! Oooh!' Nevertheless, he began untying the catch on the lid of his container. A moment later, he too had opened it cautiously. 'I suppose it must be safe,' he said, 'if you've opened up.'

Both mice got out. 'Foof!' whispered Arvee, as he shouldered his backpack. 'What a reek!'

'He's around but not very close, I think,' Ellie answered. Both mice were speaking almost into one another's ears in order to make as little noise as possible. 'I remember what it was like when he was chasing me, and it was *much* stronger.'

'He probably lives somewhere close by. D'you think I dare turn my torch on? Just a wink?'

'Tell you what,' said Ellie, 'we'll stand back-to-back and you flick your torch on for two seconds. Then we'll compare notes about what we both saw without wasting time looking around.'

'Good thinking!'

They got into position and Arvee flashed his torch. In the instant that it was lit, the mice saw that they were inside a long curving passage, not very wide or high. They pooled their impressions. 'I think the way ahead must be in front of you,' said Arvee. 'The view I had was of a lot of dead leaves.' Ellie agreed with him. 'What shall we do with these spherical torture chambers we travelled in?'

'Keep them with us, I think,' whispered Ellie. 'We should hug the walls, pushing the balls along slowly beside us. That way, if we're seen, it'll be the dung balls rather than us that'll get the first strike.'

'Remember, the snake doesn't need to *see* us,' warned Arvee. 'He's got other senses – and we'll certainly smell him long before we're close to him.'

They oriented themselves along the left-hand wall and began to move. The passage curved towards the right. As soon as they rounded the corner, the smell was stronger. Both mice stopped for a whispered consultation.

'I don't know if my eyes are playing tricks on me,' said Arvee, 'but I think I'm beginning to see a little texture in the darkness. Which means there's light leaking into this tunnel from up ahead.'

They were about to move on, when Arvee said, 'Ellie, wait! Can you hear something?'

Both mice stood very still, turning their ears this way and that.

'Yes,' she said, after a pause, 'in the distance. 'Conversation, isn't it? But we're not close enough to understand.'

'Not because we're not close – it's because it's not mouse-talk. Snakes are sort of deaf, but they pick up sounds through their other senses. They can talk to anyone who can vibrate the air in the right way.'

'Two snakes, then, do you think?' She paused. 'That'd be bad news for us all right.'

Arvee shook his head. 'No. There's only one snake. The other voice belongs to a mammal, like us. It's so odd – I can't explain why exactly I'm saying this, but . . . there's something . . . familiar about that other voice.'

'Well, we've got to keep moving. There's another corner coming up. We'll probably see and hear much more when we're round it.'

Sure enough, as they turned the next corner the dim light was more obvious. With every step they took, more details of their surroundings became visible. Simultaneously, the smell of the snake was growing heavier. The sounds of conversation were clearer too. The distinction between the two voices was apparent even to Ellie now. One a snake and the other a warm-blooded creature.

'The stench is becoming unbearable,' whispered Ellie. 'We should be able to see him very soon now – and look, the passage is widening out – and ah, look there!'

'Watch out!' Arvee grabbed Ellie, pulling her back. 'A pit, right at your feet –'

'And a snake, *there*,' breathed Ellie, as she flattened herself against the wall. Suddenly, once more, fear swamped her. Her heart was hammering against her ribs, as if it were trying to break out of there. Her legs turned to jelly and her whiskers were trembling as if she

207

were facing a strong wind. She knew she wouldn't be able to move a single millimetre forward.

They could see, in the distance, the silhouette of a decorative screen or panel against the faintly pulsing greenish light of the firefly chandeliers. Beyond the panel, they could see the head and spreading hood of the young snake. The rest of his body trailed all along the floor, with the end of his tail still inside the pit. He was facing the ornate structure and nodding submissively.

The two mice remained frozen where they were, transfixed by this tableau.

Arvee recovered before Ellie. The sound of his voice in her ears steadied her.

'OK,' he said. 'We've got to take some decisions here. This pit must be where the creature sleeps. That means, whatever else we do, we've got to get away from here before he comes back – which could be at any moment! The greatest danger for us is going to be after we're alongside that large piece of furniture. It's a throne of some kind and whoever's sitting on it isn't afraid of snakes!'

All Arvee's instincts were tingling as he said this. It was so familiar, this chamber that he had never seen before! It was as if he had visited it many times before, in dreams or in memories. He tried to shake the impression out of his mind. It was a distraction he couldn't afford just now. 'We'll need to move around the pit,' he whispered in Ellie's ear. He had felt her trembling earlier but was glad to notice she was calmer now.

'I think so,' said Ellie. 'But *who* is the snake talking to? Not a shrew, surely! Could it be Cutie? She mentioned to me that she learned Reptile.'

'I doubt it,' shrugged Arvee. 'That's not a mouse accent. Look, Ellie, I think we're going to have to split forces. Here's what I suggest. You go ahead, staying close to the wall. We're near the boundary of the garden – I can smell the bricks. I believe that suggests this chamber follows the wall, and on towards an exit. So that's the way you go – straight ahead, keeping the wall to your left – regardless of what I do. Understood? Your mission is to find Cutie. When you do, get her away from here. Got it? Just *keep going . . .*'

Ellie nodded. There was no point pretending she wanted to have anything to do with the snake. 'All right, but I have an idea. Keep both the dung balls with you.'

He understood at once, 'I can use them as potential distractions, you mean? Yes. I agree, good idea. OK, let's go.'

Moving carefully round the pit and keeping to the left, the two mice crept forward. They rolled the balls in front of them. As they neared the platform, the flooring changed to coin tiles. Now they were directly behind the dais on which the ornamental structure stood. They were still in the shadows but could see into the main space of the room. The snake was far to the right, not visible to them from where they were. Two easy chairs, a settee and a coffee table had been placed near the stacks of matchbox cabinets that lined the wall. There was ample space between the furniture and the cabinets for a mouse to move forward without being seen.

Arvee spoke into Ellie's ear. 'We should move fast now. On the count of three, I'm going to shove one dung ball forward between those two easy chairs – with me following. Meanwhile, you dash ahead, don't look back. With luck, the snake will attack the first moving thing he sees – that'll be the ball. When he realizes it's not alive, he'll flicker his tongue, locate me and then come after me. By then, you'll be in the passage ahead, and he won't even realize there are two of us.'

'But, Arvee –' began Ellie.

'We don't have time to argue!' urged Arvee. 'We're a good team – I know I can trust you and you know you can trust me.' He leaned forward and bumped noses with her. In a much softer voice he added, 'And *please* take care!'

There wasn't time to be scared either. Arvee got the first dung ball into position, then held up the three fingers of his left paw. 'Ready?' he whispered in Ellie's ear. 'On my mark, one – two – three!'

He gave the first of the light, strong spheres a powerful shove. It shot forward with a shock of energy. Simultaneously, on his left, he sensed rather than saw Ellie dash away.

The reaction from the snake was instantaneous.

As the dung ball flew towards him – ZAP! With no pause for reflection, he struck at it, his jaws gaping wide and his long, curved, poison-bearing fangs outstretched. His sinuous body snapped up in a high tight loop as his head slammed down.

In the next instant, 'OW-WOWOW!' howled the cobra. The fragile sphere had collapsed under the impact of his strike. Instead of embedding his teeth in the soft flesh of prey, he had driven them into the hard metal coins of the floor, jarring the delicate bones of his head. Venom pumped uncontrollably out of the ends of his fangs. His jaws had instinctively bitten down on the light springy mass of the sphere, squeezing the poison glands just the same as if he had struck at live prey. Meanwhile, the ball was thrust deeper into his throat, causing him to gag. 'AGHH-ACK-kkhhkkhhkkhh-ARGHH!' cried Stinky-Poo. His head began to thrash around, striking the ceiling, striking the floor and the furniture.

Arvee, however, was no longer looking at the snake.

Immediately after sending his dung ball forward, he had dashed after it. In the instant when he passed the ornate structure in the middle of the room, he looked to his right. And the final piece of the jigsaw puzzle fell into place.

'Pasha!' Arvee cried out loud, stopping in his tracks. 'Of course! You're the one behind everything!'

28

RAT-ASTROPHE!

Monday Night

Pasha had jumped to his feet, but he wasn't looking in Arvee's direction. 'Stop it!' he yelled in snake-speak. 'You fool – you'll bring this whole place down on our heads!' The sound of furniture being smashed punctuated each violent jerk of the snake's long gleaming body. Wild, fantastic shadows flew around the walls and ceiling of the audience chamber, as both the chandeliers began to swing back and forth. Bits and pieces of the decorations were coming unstuck from the plastic insulation. With low twangs, some of the bicycle spokes that braced the metal roof supports apart were springing loose too.

'Aaaghh!' cried Stinky-Poo in agony. 'Yaaaachhhh! ACCCCHHH! G-HAACKKK! G-HAACKKK-KKK-KKK!'

'He's choking,' observed Arvee, ducking to avoid a falling bottle cap. 'The ball's stuck in his throat –'

'"Ball"? What "ball"?' Pasha stopped bellowing suddenly and peered in Arvee's direction, his mouth gaping open and his eyes squinting. 'Cutie? Is that you? What're you –'

'The snake!' Arvee yelled. He jumped aside as a strip of laxatives detached itself from the ceiling with a loud ripping sound. 'He can't swallow the ball!' Nuts, bolts and screws were starting to rain down to the floor. For safety, Arvee nipped under a sturdy coffee table made from a cocktail coaster and four sawn-off chopstick ends.

'YAGHHH!' hollered the snake. 'HA-GHH! HA-KHHA-HKKK! GHA-KKKK!'

The bigger of the two chandeliers was torn loose and fell with a bump. Being made of wire, it wasn't very heavy, but the impact caused the central clip holding it together to come undone. The captive fireflies began to stream out. Green flashes swirled through the air as the flying insects searched for an exit.

'*Of course* he can't swallow – I haven't let him!' said Pasha, then yelped as a hail of washers hit him on the nose. He swatted the air with his arms, while his mute mouse attendants cowered under the overhanging sections of his throne. He bellowed once more at the serpent. 'Stop flinging yourself about, you ridiculous tadpole – and . . . TAKE IT! Did you hear me? TAKE IT, I said, TAKE IT!'

It wasn't immediate, but by the fourth or fifth time Pasha had repeated the crucial phrase, Stinky-Poo began to calm down. He retracted his hood and instead of struggling against the obstruction in his throat, concentrated on making it as compact as he could manage while simultaneously swallowing hard.

In a very short while, the situation was under control. There was a large lump in the snake's neck, but his mouth was shut, and he was breathing properly, no longer heaving his body about.

The audience chamber, however, was a shambles. The sturdy metal hoops that supported the plastic insulation were still in place, but the roof was sagging in several places where the bicycle spokes had come loose. Shards of broken furniture lay everywhere. The second chandelier was listing to one side. The floor was littered with glittering bits of metal. Fireflies blinked and jittered in the air.

Pasha was so furious he couldn't speak for several seconds. He was bleeding from the nose, his lips were drawn back from his sharp yellow teeth and his chest was heaving. Then a last copper bolt fell from the ceiling.

It hit his turban, which came undone, covering his face in a veil of crumpled pink chiffon. 'Arrrhhh!' he snarled in frustration, tearing the cloth away. His dark fur was standing up in a thick ridge that ran from between his brows down the back of his neck. His poor damaged eyes were rolling in their sockets, as he tried to focus on Stinky-Poo.

'You – you clumsy, brainless *earthworm*!' he said finally, in snake-speak.

He took a step forward, as if intending to climb down from his platform. One of the mute mice came forward from where he'd been hiding to help the rat. But Pasha flung him aside with such force that the little creature struck his head against the side of the throne and was knocked out. A second mute mouse was about to go forward, but her companion stopped her. A glance passed between them. Instead of going to Pasha, they went to the aid of their fallen companion.

'You've destroyed my beautiful room!' raved the rat. 'My priceless collection of artefacts – saved from the Flood at such expense! Aarrhhhhh! My treasures! My trophies!' With one foot, he felt for the edge of the platform and, finding it, took a step down. 'I should have realized that you were too foolish, too ignorant and witless, to be worth teaming up with! I should have left you in the gutter, with your stink and your misery. Hungry, are you? HAH!' He got down the second step.

'I'll show you hunger! Down – put your stupid head DOWN! That's right, on the floor – not another hiss from you!' He had reached the third step.

Arvee understood just enough Reptile to be astounded at Pasha's audacity. How did he, a prey species, dare to address a predator as dangerous as a cobra in such a tone of voice? More astounding still was the snake's response.

His head on the floor, he said, 'No, Ma*th*ter! Plea*the*, Ma*th*ter,' in the most humble tone. 'Don't say the Word! Plea*the* don't. Plea*the*! I'm really, *th*eriou*th*ly *th*tarving. I had a headache already and now I've *th*pilled my venom by mi*th*take and bumped my fang*th*! I'll never get any *th*leep tonight, I ju*th*t know it. If I don't get *th*ome*th*ing to eat *th*oon, I – I'll – faint!'

'Don't be an idiot, you idiot!' screamed Pasha. 'Snakes don't *th*ipill – uh – spill their venom by mistake.'

'No, Ma*th*ter, we can, and I did. Ju*th*t now,' the snake was saying. 'While trying to *th*wallow that ball. It'*th* eck*th*remely embarra*th*ing for me. But it did happen. And I –'

A jolt ran up Arvee's spine as he crouched under the table – something had touched him! In the next instant, he relaxed. It was Ellie. She had evidently crept up alongside him so quietly that he hadn't noticed. 'It's me,' she whispered now, in his ear. 'We're both here, Cutie and I.'

Cutie came up along Arvee's other side. 'Hi, Arvee! It's me, Cutie.'

'Cutie! Ellie!' exclaimed Arvee under his breath. 'What're you two doing here?'

'Oh, come on, Arvee!' she scolded. 'No way we'd leave you alone to face Pasha!'

'Besides,' said Ellie, 'Cutie's fluent in Reptile. She's been translating.'

'There's a word Pasha uses,' explained Cutie now, 'to keep Stinky-Poo – that's the snake – under hypnotic control. If we hear it, we can say it too. That way, we can stop him from eating us, whenever we like.'

All three mice remained very still, straining their ears to listen.

'Never mind!' shrieked Pasha, 'I don't care about your finer feelings, your neurotic fits, your lack of self-esteem!' He took a step forward. 'I'm through with you, do you understand, you animated garden hose? To imagine I had such high hopes, when I first met you, of our partnership, unique in the entire animal kingdom! With my cunning and your fear-inspiring presence, together we could have ruled this place! We could have been kings, emperors! But instead, what did I get? Mindless, worthless fuss.' He parodied the snake's manner. ' "No, Ma*th*ter, I don't like frightening the mi*th*e. No, Ma*th*ter, I'm not in the mood for a cha*th*e. No-thi*th*, no-that, no-the-other!" Well, I'm tired of it! I'm going to fix you once and for all. I'm going to say the Word, and NEVER UNDO IT!' He laughed maniacally.

Stinky-Poo shrank back, pleading pathetically. 'Plea*the*, Ma*th*ter – don't, don't –'

Pasha laughed nastily again. 'You just try and stop me!' He took another step forward – and fell flat on his nose. There was a thud, accompanied by a sticky splash. 'YAAAAAHHH!' he roared. 'WHAT'S THIS . . . GOOP on the floor?'

There was a silence. Then, in a very different voice, this time breathless with fear, he said, 'W-wait. . . it's not. . . not. . . *venom*, is it?' No one answered him. 'P-p-please-ease-ease!' he whispered hoarsely. 'S-s-someone . . . s-s-save . . . save . . . m-m-m-m-me . . . p-please . . .' His voice failed, and he was no longer able to speak. He began to drag himself away from where the poisonous liquid pool lay.

'We've got to help him,' said Arvee, starting to crawl out from under the coffee table.

'Wait,' said Ellie, as she got up. She helped Cutie up too.

The three mute mouse attendants were standing between Pasha's fallen body and the coffee table where Arvee, Ellie and Cutie had been hidden. In the intermittent flashes of light produced by the fireflies, their faces were visible. They had their ears folded back. Their paws were held up, palms forward, clearly signalling that they didn't intend to let anyone come to the rat's aid. 'No,' their expressions said. 'We've had enough. The tyrant is finally dying. Let him go.'

Arvee would have moved forward anyway, but Ellie held him back. 'Arvee,' she said, 'there's nothing we *can* do for him. He had a cut on his nose. The venom will have got to his bloodstream by now. It's hopeless.'

There was a slipping, sliding, slithering sound as Stinky-Poo swayed forward. The three mouse attendants jumped around, sinking to the ground, their whiskers trembling. But they did not move away. Arvee marvelled at their courage.

'What i*th* wrong with the Ma*th*ter?' asked Stinky-Poo. 'Why i*th* he moving *th*o *th*trangely?'

Pasha was continuing to crawl away. He had reached the far side of the platform.

'I*th* it becau*the* of *th*omething I did?' The snake turned to look at the gathered mice. He was surprised to notice that there seemed to be more than ever before. He flickered his tongue delicately at them, trying to gather vital information about them through the sense organs in his tongue: yes, they were all breathing and alive, even the one who was lying a short distance away. He appeared to be asleep. But these others were perfectly awake. Their hearts were beating rather fast and their bodies were deliciously warm. His stomach gave a painful groan. 'Oh dear,' he hissed softly. 'I'm really *th*o hungry . . .' His tongue flickered again. 'You're all edible, I hope?'

29

FAST-FOOD EXPRESS!

Monday Midnight

There was a strange silence as the same four thoughts raced around and around in the minds of all six mice. The seventh was still knocked out. 'None of us knows the Word to stop him eating us!', 'He's a very hungry snake!', 'I'd better get out of his way RIGHT NOW!' and 'Whoever gets left behind will be eaten.'

But Arvee whispered urgently to Cutie, 'Quick! Can you be my interpreter?'

Cutie whispered back, 'Sure, but –'

'Just do it, please. Say, "Yes, we are edible."'

Cutie did as she was asked.

Stinky-Poo perked up at once. 'Oh! Do you know my language? That'*th tho* cool! If only I wa*th*n't *tho* hungry, I'd love to chat!'

Arvee said, through Cutie, 'I think I can help out with your hunger.'

'Oh, wow!' said the snake. 'That'*th* ama*th*ing! No prey ha*th* ever *th*aid that to me before!' His head shot forward and Arvee had to grab Ellie and Cutie on either side of him to stop them from jumping back. That would have been fatal, he knew: the cobra would have struck instinctively, as he had done with the dung ball, at any moving thing. 'Are you *th*ure?'

'Ah-ah,' said Arvee, 'not so fast! I wasn't offering myself, you know!'

'No?' said Stinky-Poo, cocking his head to one side. He sounded disappointed. 'That'*th* a *th*hame. I wa*th* looking forward to eating *th*omeone who actually offered him*th*elf to me. You have NO idea how *th*ad it i*th* to alway*th* be cha*th*ing after one'*th* food! How about one of your friend*th*, then? I'll be very quick, I promi*the*. It won't hurt at all.'

There was a collective squeak from the other mice. 'Umm . . . no,' said Arvee, through Cutie, who, like any professional translator, included the pause. 'What I had in mind was something completely different. A sort of invention of mine.' He removed his arms from round the other two mice as he talked, hoping that they had the good sense not to make any sudden moves. He shrugged his backpack off his shoulders. 'If you'll just wait a minute, I'll get it out.'

'You brought a *th*nack for me?' said Stinky-Poo. 'That'*th* really more kind than anyone ha*th* been to me before!'

Both Cutie and Ellie were staring at Arvee in concern. Ellie whispered, 'Arvee? You *do* realize he can only eat live prey?'

'Well,' said Arvee to Stinky-Poo, 'like I said, this is a bit of an experiment. Now, if you don't mind, Mr Cobra, sir, please back away and give me some room.' He started to unzip his backpack.

'*Th*ure, *th*ure,' said the snake, immediately flowing his body back till he was well away. 'Anything you *th*ay. I do hope it doe*th*n't *th*queak too loudly though – bad for my nerve*th*, you know – alway*th* give*th* me a *th*tomach up*th*et.'

'In that case,' said Arvee reasonably, as he fiddled with something inside the backpack, 'your stomach must be upset more often than not?'

'It i*th*,' said Stinky-Poo, with a feeling-filled sigh. 'It may be the rea*th*on I have thi*th* awful *th*mell.'

'OK,' said Arvee to Ellie, Cutie and the other mice. 'This is going to be a bit of shock for everyone, so if you'd prefer, please close your eyes.'

'Oh, my whiskers!' said Ellie, with her eyes shut. 'I smell pepperoni.'

'But that isn't –' Cutie started to say.

There was a buzzing, whirring sound and then something hummed and moved forward. Arvee had tied a large lump of spicy sausage down on to one of his miniature radio-controlled toy cars. Though the toy was small enough for a young mouse to play with, it was surprisingly powerful. Using the remote-unit in his hand, he pressed a button. The tiny food-laden vehicle shot towards Stinky-Poo.

' – alive!' finished Cutie, opening her eyes in surprise.

'Ooohh!' exclaimed the cobra, as something small and dark zoomed at him. 'What I*TH* that? I've never *th*een anything like it be –' THWAP! He struck it and GLOMP! – a moment later, had swallowed it. '. . . fore!' he finished his word. 'Mmm. *Th*trange flavour. Never ta*th*ted anything like it *th*o far.' He looked towards Arvee with new respect, 'Intere*th*ting! Do you have any more?'

'Sorry, no,' said Arvee. 'Tell you what, though – I can get more, if you'll let us go now.' He held his breath. This was the crucial moment. He could see the lump of pepperoni making its way down the snake's throat. The toy car was probably small enough to pass through the creature's gut without difficulties, just like the indigestible fur and bones of his normal food. However, there was a possibility that the oily, spicy sausage would upset a reptilian stomach. Whereupon the snake would throw up and be twice as hungry.

But Stinky-Poo was bobbing and curtsying, speechless with strong emotions. When he could finally talk again, he said, 'You know, thi*th* i*th* the very, very fir*tht* time that anyone ha*th* been *tho* kind to me. Of cour*the* you can all go.' Cutie immediately relaxed and gave the others a thumbs-up sign. Everyone grinned in relief. 'Your *th*nack will keep me going for a little while, and then maybe I . . .' He faltered. 'If there*'th th*omething wrong with the Ma*th*ter, I *th*uppo*the* I'll have to do my own hunting again, won't I?' He gave a big sigh. 'I'll ju*tht* have to go back to *th*tarving again, in which ca*the*.'

Arvee, daring greatly, said, 'Uh, well, if you tell us what the problem is . . . maybe we can help? I'm sort of good at finding solutions.'

The snake said, in a mournful voice, 'It'*th* my *th*think, don't you *th*ee? I can't creep up on any prey, 'cau*the* they alway*th th*mell me before I can get to them. That'*th* how I got involved with the Ma*th*ter in the fir*tht* pla*the*. I tried *th*neaking up on him, but he *th*melt me and hid from me. Then he told me he could cure me of my problem, if I would let him hypnoti*the* me. Of cour*the*, I *th*aid ye*th*. After that, I COULDN'T eat unle*th* he allowed me.' He sighed again. 'It'*th* very *th*ad being me.'

'My whiskers!' said Arvee. 'I'd forgotten about the smell entirely!' He sniffed the air, then looked surprised. Then amazed. 'Wait a minute!' He called for the attention of the other mice. 'Everyone – one moment – smell the air. Am I imagining it? Or is it less smelly down here?'

It was. All the mice confirmed it. 'No! It i*th*n't POT*HI*BLE!' Stinky-Poo cried. 'I can't believe it! Really? I don't *th*mell any more?' He tossed his head this way and that. He seemed overwhelmed with joy.

His whole body wriggled and coiled in graceful loops. 'Oh, my! Oh, what a fabulou*th* feeling! It'*th* true! I can actually *th*mell *th*omething el*th*e for a change! Oh! Oh!'

Though there was still a taint in the air, the dreadful odour of decay and doom that had characterized Stinky-Poo's presence so far was definitely on the wane. From being something that couldn't be ignored for even a second, it had become a background feature.

He turned towards Arvee with the closest thing to a smile that his stiff, rather rigid snake's face could manage. '*Th*ir, I don't know your name, but I'm beginning to think you mu*th*t be a magi*th*ian of *th*ome *th*ort. How did you do it? I can't tell you how grateful I am . . . Finally, I can leave thi*th* pla*th*e and get a life! Maybe even *th*top feeling hungry all the time.'

He laid his big, scaly head down on the floor in front of Arvee. At such close quarters, the astonishing geometry and smooth perfection of his scales were very striking. Looking straight into the snake's lidless eyes, Arvee was surprised to notice that they were just like anyone else's. Full of intelligence, wit and personality. Somehow, this made it much easier to stop fearing the creature.

'I don't have any gift*th* to give anyone,' whispered Stinky-Poo. 'Never had any friend*th*, after all. *Th*till, there i*th* one thing I can think of giving you. *Th*ome-thing in eck*th*ange for what you've done for me, and that i*th* . . .' He paused and swallowed nervously. This was the second time in his life that he was offering anyone such trust. He hoped this time would turn out to be better than the previous one. 'And that i*th* the Word. The Word that'll *th*top me from *th*wallowing. In ca*th*e I, you know, at *th*ome future time, uhhh . . .'

Arvee nodded at once, in understanding. 'Of course,' he said, 'in case you suffer an uncontrollable urge in friendly company.'

The snake brought his head closer and said the Word carefully. It was composed of three separate syllables which he pronounced in reverse order, to avoid accidentally hypnotizing himself while saying it. 'Up . . . It. . . Shut,' he said. 'Up-It-Shut.'

'I am deeply honoured,' said Arvee, memorizing it the correct way, SHUT-IT-UP, taking care not to say it out aloud. He was very touched that the cobra would trust him with such powerful knowledge. More than ever, he was conscious of the sensitive nature of the snake. It was something that would never have occurred to him before this night.

'OK,' said Stinky-Poo. 'And now I'll tell you what to *th*ay to relea*th*e me.'

'I know that already,' said Arvee. 'It's what Pasha said when you were choking on the – A-HA!' he exclaimed, so loudly that Stinky-Poo sprang back and flared his hood in fright. All the other mice jumped.

'Dung ball!' cried Arvee. 'Neem! The dung ball was made from the bark of the neem tree – which has medicinal properties – and that's what cured your stink, I bet!'

'Wow,' said the snake, in a hushed voice. 'I never thought it wa*th* po*th*ible . .

'Well, that's miraculous!' grinned Ellie. 'I came in here thinking I might never see daylight again, and now –'

But she was interrupted by the sound of ugly laughter.

'And now, NOTHING! You still won't see daylight, silly dimwit!' The dark, rich voice of Pasha was unmistakable. All the gathered mice and Stinky-Poo looked around as his laughter rang out again. 'Stupid, bumbling, overconfident little mice! Don't you ever understand that you can't win against a superior animal like me? Ha-ha-ha-ha-ha-ha!' He was across from where all the mice and Stinky-Poo were now bunched, moving slowly forward. He was pushing something in front of him. It was about the size of a large square cupboard, but made of wire, and set on Lego-wheels.

'There's something I never told you, Dr Smarty-Pants Arvee, in those happy days we spent together in Ratland. Something you might find hard to believe. Here it is. I grew up in a Laboratory too! I was an ordinary rat, of course, not a freakish albino. But I was destined for glory. They did experiments on me. I never got around to telling any of you about those, did I? Well, let me tell you now. They were to test resistance to . . . you guessed it! Cobra venom.' He laughed wickedly again. 'Human scientists dosed me with the deadly poison, increasing the amount little by little. When they thought I'd reached my limit, they gave me a parting shot to kill me. Then they threw me out on the discard pile. Cruel? Yes. But I survived. And the venom left me stronger and healthier than ever before. So they did me a favour, the humans, without intending to.'

He had come to a halt under the remaining chandelier. Inside the wire-frame shelf that he had been pushing in front of him were a number of small, rounded shapes. 'I never forgot the lesson I learned in the Lab – not reading, not writing, not science or geography. Only . . . SURVIVAL. That's everything. When you mice destroyed my gorgeous home in the old building, it was a terrible blow to me, yes. But did I let it vanquish me? Never! Not me. All the others ran away, my brave and stupid followers. But I picked myself up, healed my wounds and . . . swore to get my revenge. Well, here it is.' He invited the others to come forward. 'Gather round, you pathetic tadpoles! And take a look at the trump card I've had up my sleeve all along. The answer to all your dreams . . . and the price of all your nightmares.'

The mute mouse attendants were standing in a huddle. They knew what was in the wire shelves. Stinky-Poo hadn't been able to understand the conversation of the animals in the room. He kept his distance from the rat, nervously coiling and uncoiling the length of his body. But Arvee, Ellie and Cutie stepped forward. It took them a few seconds to realize what they were looking at.

Arvee was the first to speak. 'Oh,' he whispered. 'Oh . . . my . . . whiskers!' He looked at Pasha with horror and disgust in his eyes. 'I never realized what the true meaning of a monster was until this moment.'

30

TRAPPED

Monday Post-midnight

The small rounded shapes inside the individual coops of the wire shelf were baby mice. They were alive but emaciated and grimy. Their eyes were shut and their breathing was shallow.

'Spider toxin,' said Pasha. 'They're in suspended animation, just like the ants.'

Ellie turned on the rat, fury in her eyes. 'How . . . how *could* you? I know the parents of some of these little ones!'

'Wonderful! They're going to be *so* thrilled to find that their beloved larvae are alive!' countered Pasha. 'So grateful to get them back that they'll be willing, I bet, to give up every possession, every gram of pride, every last iota of their so-called precious independence, to have their young ones home once more!'

'Oooh!' cried Cutie. 'You horrid, nasty BULLY!' She flexed her muscles and called to the others, 'Come on, team! We can take him on, we can knock the stuffing out of him!' And she advanced on the rat, legs kicking, paws and arms slashing at the air in classic taekwondo manoeuvres.

But Arvee caught her. 'No, Cutie. He's made sure we won't try to harm him.'

Pasha's smirk stretched from ear to ear. 'How well you understand me, Dr Arvee.'

'Let me go!' squeaked Cutie, struggling. 'I can take him on. I can bash him up.'

'No,' said Arvee. His expression was sombre. 'Because of the babies. Unlike the ants, they'll need an antidote stronger than honey. And only Pasha knows what that antidote is. So he'll hold us all to ransom. For the sake of these unfortunate mites.'

Pasha nodded his huge head. 'Oh, Doctor, how like me you are! Just think – with our combined brains, yours and mine, we could have ruled the world. But you're *too sensitive* to want mere power, aren't you? Had to ally yourself with the downtrodden masses, didn't you? Ho, yes! Well. You see how it's worked out in the end? Either you become my personal slave and the squeakers go free or . . . you snuff me out, and lose these darling little furballs too! Dearie me, haha-hahah! What a sad and tragic fate – aaahahahahaha!' He threw his head back and roared. 'You'll have to admit, you ruby-eyed albino freak, it's a checkmate worthy of the grandest of grand masters! Oh, yes! Oh, very yessy-yes!'

Stinky-Poo, who had been hanging back all this while, slithered forward suddenly. 'Ma*th*ter?' he said, raising his hood up timidly, 'I'm *th*orry, I hate to bother you at a time like thi*th*. I don't under*thth*and what all of you are *th*aying, and it look*th* a*th* if it'*th* very important. But –'

Pasha whirled around towards the snake. 'Get back!' he snarled. 'Not another word from you, you snivelling ectotherm! You trashed my audience chamber and now you've befriended the stupid mice!'

'Ma*th*ter, Ma*th*ter,' said the snake, plaintively. 'Plea*the* – I ju*th*t want to point out that –'

'Nothing!' screamed Pasha. 'Not another hiss! Not another slurred syllable!' He had risen up to his fullest height. 'Get away from me – go on – scat! Yaah!' he said, raising his arm to give the snake a punch on his snout. But there was an ominous, twanging, ripping, scraping sound from overhead. The sleeve of Pasha's robe was caught in the second firefly chandelier hanging crookedly from a loosened bicycle spoke just above him. Irritably, not realizing what he risked, he jerked his arm forward. And the whole glittering, pulsating construction came down over his head.

The clip holding the wire construction together came loose. Fireflies began to stream out of their confinement as the rat struggled within a tangled mass of metal.

'The light looked like it wa*th* going to fall,' said Stinky-Poo. He had jumped back just in time to avoid being hit by the chandelier. 'And it ha*th*,' he said, rather unnecessarily.

But '*Hraaack!*' was all that Pasha could say as he floundered and struck out at the wire cage that held him fast in its grip.

'What's the matter with him?' said Ellie.

'Look!' said Cutie. 'He . . . he seems to be lit up from inside!'

It was true. Some fireflies, in their bid to escape, had flown straight down the rat's gaping mouth as the chandelier collapsed around him. '*Ngggaaaaah! H'ghaaaak!*' croaked Pasha as he tore at his clothes. '*H'ghaaaack* me! *H'ghaaaack* me!' He flailed with his arms, he kicked with his feet. But the fireflies were stuck tight in his gullet and down his windpipe. They flashed greenish-red from within the rat's heaving chest, lighting up his internal organs so that he looked like a macabre living lamp.

'Quick, quick!' said Arvee, dashing forward, even as the blink-blink-blink-a-blinking cloud of fireflies flew excitedly around, once again turning the room into a carousel of swirling shadows and green light. 'Come on, everyone, we'll have to pull this wire thing off him.'

But there wasn't enough time. The mice tugged and pulled at the outermost of the wires in vain. From within the collapsed frame of the chandelier, the rat's rattling gasps were heard. *'H'roooohi!'* he cried. *'H'gg-ahhhar-hic! Haaa-kkk!* G-gggg-g-ggg. Hmmoo. Hhh. Hm.' His twitching movements slowed to a halt. The black quivering mass of his whiskers stopped moving. With fireflies still pulsing and whirling up from the wreckage of the great light, Pasha's huge body shuddered twice and he died.

'Oh, no,' said Arvee, in a hushed whisper. 'The babies . . .'

The three mice clung to one another, too shocked and dazed to move. Stinky-Poo was swaying this way and that close by. He felt sure that something or other was his fault – it usually was – but he couldn't for the life of him figure out what it was.

'Well,' said Ellie in a dull voice eventually, 'we'd best be going then.' Every nerve felt as if it had been scraped with a rusty blade. She turned.

Just behind her, but at a respectful distance, stood one of the mute mouse attendants, holding something in her paws. The other three attendants, including the one who had been knocked out, were standing near the wire shelf containing the unconscious mouse babies.

'They want to give us something,' said Cutie, who had grown expert at interpreting the mute mice. 'It's . . .' She took the corked vial from the attendant. Inside the vial, which had been made from the hollowed bulb of a torch, was a pale fluid.

Cutie opened the small container and took a sniff. When she turned to the others, it was with an excited, wondering edge to her voice. 'Hey, team, I can't be sure – I did only one course in toxicology after all – but I'm willing to bet my false eyelashes that this is the antidote to the spider toxin!' She grinned as she thumped the mouse attendant on her shoulder. 'Great work! Now let's all go up and celebrate.'

31

ANYTHING'S POSSIBLE

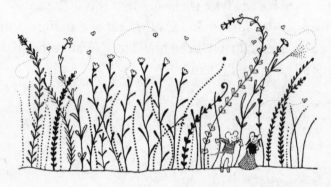

One Week Later

There had been a brief rainstorm during the day. Now that night had fallen, steam was rising off the earth as it cooled down. Arvee and Ellie were strolling through the tall grass near Lantana Enclave. Each blade was seamed with diamond drops of rain. Twirling veils of mist eddied round the two mice. Far above, the night sky was spangled with stars.

'Cutie's agreed to my division of the house,' Arvee was saying. 'She's OK with the idea that we can share the house just as friends, without being engaged. There's certainly enough room in *Mercara*.'

Ellie's whiskers twitched. 'That's true enough.'

'Yes,' said Arvee. 'We're both scholars, she said, and we both need our solitude and our own space. She'll continue living in the guest room, with a rope ladder to her window so that she can come and go as she pleases, and . . . Why are you grinning like that?'

'Oh, nothing,' said Ellie.

'Out with it – I can see you're holding something back.'

'Who, me? Not at all!' said Ellie. 'It's just that I noticed, the last time I spoke to her, how often the name "Toon" cropped up in her conversation . . .'

'Huh?' said Arvee, scratching his nose. 'I don't understand. What's that got to do with her accepting the division of the house?'

'Don't tie your tail in knots puzzling over it,' teased Ellie. 'Let me tell you instead about the latest development with the shrews . . .'

Their walk had taken them past the site of what had been called the Platform of Truth just one week ago. It was currently swarming with mice and a few curious beetles. A major construction project was under way, with a plan to turn the whole area into an underground museum. It would include artefacts from the Ratland era as well as the recent troubles, now referred to as the Age of Repression. Pasha's body had been placed in a casque and sealed behind a wall. Curious visitors could hear an oral history of the rat's unusual life and death by feeding sugar crystals to the recorder ants, who took turns performing this service. There was to be a gallery at which designers such as Stringer and others could show off their latest creations, a school for teaching young mice basic skills and a restaurant serving the latest innovations in mouse cuisine.

'Apart from going back to the kitchen garden,' said Ellie, 'the shrews have agreed to talks about how both communities, ours and theirs, can live in this garden without conflict. The garden lizards have mental records going back several decades to show that the garden belongs to everybody. No single species can occupy some part of it exclusively or make decisions about how to live in it without everyone's consent.'

'That sounds great,' said Arvee, his pink eyes lighting up. 'This garden can be a wonderful place when we're all at peace.'

Though it was night, everyone was out, wearing bright colourful clothes again. Children were climbing the upper reaches of the lantana bushes and all the girl mice had lantana florets in their hair.

'D'you want to come home for dinner?' asked Ellie, as they watched all the activity.

'I'd love that,' said Arvee. 'Also, there's a project I'd like to discuss with Ding, if she's interested. But I'd like to run it past you first. It's a bit bizarre.'

'Why am I not surprised?' smiled Ellie.

'As you know,' said Arvee, 'Stinky-Poo and I have remained in touch – I've been feeding him my so-called "dead-prey" preparations – tying food on to remote-controlled cars and letting him catch them as if they were living things. I believe the reason he needs live prey is that his gastric juices aren't released unless he thinks he's chasing something. So, as long as he can pretend that's what's happening, he can eat. This is probably the first time ever that a snake has been fed artificially! I'm feeling so encouraged by his response that I want to take him to a new level of nutrition.'

'Wait a minute. Aren't you running out of toy cars?' asked Ellie. 'I know you brought a number of them, but . . .'

Arvee smoothed back his whiskers. 'I won't go into the messy details, but let's just say the recycling effort has been quite successful! I wrap the cars in foil, and that protects them from damage while they're, uhhh, being "processed".'

'Oh, my!' said Ellie, holding her nose with hands. 'Sounds *smelly*! I'm not sure I want to hear what plans you have for the "new" level!'

'You'll approve, I think. But I'll need your mum's help. I need someone with an expert knowledge of food and nutrition. To devise a vegetarian diet. For a snake.'

Ellie gazed at him in amazement. 'Do you think it's *possible*?' she asked. 'Doesn't it go against the laws of nature and all that?'

'Anything's possible,' said Arvee. 'Shall I give you another example?'

'Try me,' said Ellie.

'Stinky-Poo's new living quarters. You won't believe who he's living with now!'

Ellie wrinkled her brow. 'Uh . . . tell me?'

'Mr "Hunter" Bangle, the mongoose!' said Arvee, delighted at having something really fur-ruffling to share with Ellie. 'It seems they share an interest in insect rhythms and dandelion wine. Stinky-Poo's thrilled to bits. He says he really prefers the company of warm-blooded animals, especially when he doesn't have to worry that he might accidentally eat them. I tell you, that snake is a real freethinker. He simply ignores any laws of nature that don't interest him.'

'You're making it up, Arvee!' cried Ellie. 'A cobra living with a mongoose? Now I've heard everything.' They started walking towards her home. 'Next you'll be telling me that mice could grow wings if they wanted!'

'Hmmm!' said Arvee. 'Not a bad idea at all. Just think, we'd be able to fly back and forth between *Mercara* and Lantana, with no need of those pesky Mantis Airline flights.'

'In your dreams, Arvee,' said Ellie, tucking her arm into his fondly. 'And mine too.'

ACKNOWLEDGEMENTS

Warm thanks to:

Polly Nolan, for her warm and sensitive editing on *Mouse Attack* and for commissioning the sequel *Mouse Invaders*, both first published by Macmillan Children's Books (UK).

Kate Shaw, who agented *Mouse Attack* and *Mouse Invaders*.

Thomas Abraham, for being willing to consider republishing both these titles.

Vatsala Kaul Banerjee, for her warm, firm and always-sensible editorial support, while bringing Arvee and friends to the Indian market in a local edition.

Meena Rajasekaran, for her friendly and patient collaboration, using my drawings in her cover design.

Also available from Hachette India Children's Books

THINGS BEGIN TO HAPPEN WHEN THERE'S A SMART MOUSE IN THE HOUSE!

Arvee, a clever and scholarly mouse, is horrified to find that he must leave his laboratory to live as a house pet. His new home, Paradise Villa, is charming and comfortable but *boring*. And lonely.

All that changes when Arvee meets bright, feisty Ellie and the rest of her family of house mice. They tell him about Pasha, a huge, fearsome rat who, along with his thugs, has taken over Paradise Villa, harassing and enslaving the mice. A small, brave band of rebels is ready to fight back. But how?

Arvee brings his thinking skills to the struggle, pulling in the help of other house creatures. But Pasha has very different plans for him. And Alphonso the cat is not too far behind either.

Will Arvee succeed in helping Ellie, her family and all the other mice under attack?